ALL I WANT FOR CHRISTMAS IS NOT YOU

J. S. COOPER
NATALIA LAMB

Copyright © 2023 by J. S. Cooper

All rights reserved.

No part of this book may be reproduced in any form or by any electronic or mechanical means, including information storage and retrieval systems, without written permission from the author, except for the use of brief quotations in a book review.

To everyone that has ever had a crush on someone they thought was unattainable. This one is for you!

BLURB

Can you imagine having a one-night stand with the one guy you absolutely cannot stand?

Trust me when I say you do not want to make the same mistake that I did.

His name is Colton.

Colton Hart.

He's my brother's best friend.

My nemesis.

The man who fired me after I worked for him for one hour.

Now, he's my latest mistake.

And it's all the fault of my best friend Isabel and her spiked eggnog.

And the masks.

And that one slow dance at my brother's work party that got me all hot and bothered.

I didn't know it was him.

Not until we were outside, pressed against the wall, devouring each other.

He doesn't believe I didn't realize it was him at first.

The next morning, my brother found me in his bedroom.

With Colton's boxers in my hand. FML!

So I pretended I was there to do his laundry as his new assistant.

Colton's smirk tells me that he thinks that this is something I've always wanted.

But it's not true.

I do not want Colton Hart.

In fact, all I want for Christmas is not him.

1

Dear Diary,

It's three weeks until Christmas. Am I being too greedy if I ask Santa for a hot man, a.k.a. Tom Brady, a billion dollars, and a new car? Also, if he magically makes thirty pounds disappear from my body, I won't hate him.

If you hadn't guessed it, life is not going as planned. I just lost my job, I have no boyfriend, no potential boyfriend, no Chanel handbag, no MFA applications completed, and none of my posts on Instagram for my artwork have gone viral.

I'm not going to say I'm a loser because I'm not...most of the time. I'm manifesting good things for the evening. I'm going to my brother's work party with Isabel, and then we're going to make the rounds of all the bars on the Lower East Side. Maybe I'll meet a hot banker who wants to make me the new housewife of NYC. We'll see.

Toodle-oo.

Ella

P.S. If my future hubby can be good in bed as well, I'd

really appreciate it. I don't want to have to explain to him that a quick rub is not all it takes. :P

There is a sense of excitement in the air as I look around the crowded room. I don't know who anyone is other than Isabel, and I don't really care. Tonight, I'm glad to be the sexy, anonymous, twenty-four-year-old butterfly as opposed to the slightly depressed, just-been-fired doormat that I've been the last week. However, I am not going to think about the drama of the previous days. Instead, I am going to focus on the promise of the night ahead.

"Don't look now, but that guy with the gold mask is staring at you." My best friend Isabel can't contain the excitement in her voice. "He's looking at you like he wants to eat you." She raises her voice slightly so I can hear her over the Mariah Carey song that's playing through the speakers in the large conference room.

"Who?" I look around unabashedly to see if he's cute. Not that I'll see his face, but at least I'll be able to check out his body and see if he's my type or not. I adjust the silver mask on my face so that the feathers aren't completely covering my eyes.

The room is dark, with silver mirror balls on the ceiling and flashing strobe lights. We're meant to feel like we're in a trendy bar and not the law offices of Parker and Parker, Attorneys at Law. Whoever the party planner is has done a good job. Even if there are kitsch statues of reindeer and Santa Claus sprinkled around the room. It's Christmas, so the cheap holiday decor is forgiven. Plus, I love Christmas decorations. It is my favorite time of year. And not even being fired can stop that feeling of festive joy running down my spine.

"I told you not to look, Ella." Isabel shakes her head but grins widely. She knows me well enough to know that there is no way I'm not going to look after what she said.

Especially seeing as the unknown guy won't even know I'm looking at him. If he does somehow realize I'm checking him out, he won't know who I am. Just as I won't know who he is.

Because one, this is my brother's work party, and I barely know anyone here, and two, I am wearing a mask covering half of my face. As is everyone else at this shindig.

If I'm honest, I think it is weird for a law firm to have an office Christmas party that is reminiscent of a scene at a sex club, but it wasn't like I made the decision to go with the dominatrix club theme.

I have no idea which member of the firm came up with the "Eyes Wide Shut" Christmas party theme, but I'm not hating it. It allows Isabel and me to dress super sexy without feeling like sluts. Not that we ever feel that way normally. However, when we leave the party later to go clubbing, we'll have a reason for the masks on our faces.

Isabel and I are only here for the free booze and food and the opportunity to win some cool presents in the Secret Santa. Sure, we don't actually work here and, as such, most probably shouldn't enter the Secret Santa, but who's to know besides HR? And they are too busy trying to make sure that none of the partners get busted for sexual harassment. You'd be amazed at how many upper-level executives use holiday parties to cop a feel of their secretaries.

My older brother, Sam, invited us as he knows that we both love a good party. And it isn't like we've come empty-handed and expect to go home with something. We did bring presents for the exchange. We'd both gone to Dollar General and bought items we'd gift-wrapped to exchange.

Some may say it's unfair to spend five dollars and walk away with a present worth up to five hundred dollars (thanks, rich law firm partners), but I just call it the balance and equalization of life.

I look around to see if anyone is gazing my way, and

that's when I see him. Tall, dark, and handsome. Granted, the light is low in the room, and I can't see his face properly, but the suit this man is wearing clings to him like it doesn't want to leave his muscular body. I wave my fingers at him with all the confidence of a woman who knows she looks hot at that moment, and he waves back before I turn back to Isabel.

"He looks hot." I giggle, my face flushed. It's been over a year since I've been on a date. And even longer since I've slept with anyone. Not that this is the event to pick up a guy to sleep with. My brother would kill me if I hooked up with someone from his firm. Especially one of the partners. Not that I know if Pin-Striped Suit is a partner or not. Not that I care, either.

It's not like I came to the party with the intent to hook up with a hottie. I'm not normally even attracted to lawyers and suits. I'm much more into the tormented artist sort of guy. The ones that write you a poem and sing you a song on their guitar at midnight and tell you how misunderstood they are. And even then I don't hook up right away.

I'm not that sort of girl.

"Let's get this party started." Isabel hands me a cup of something alcoholic, and I take it gratefully. I haven't had a drink in weeks, and I'm in the mood to have some fun. This week hasn't been great for me. I'd been fired from another admin job. This time, it really hadn't been my fault. I'd questioned my boss when he'd asked me to submit a five-hundred-dollar hotel stay to his work expenses, and he'd felt like I'd been asking too many questions. How was I to know that he'd taken his mistress to the hotel and was suspicious that I was a plant working for his wife?

"This tastes good," I say as I down the contents of the glass. "Eggnog?" I ask as I swing my hips to the beat of the music. Who doesn't love Mariah at a Christmas party? I'm even starting to feel festive. The party organizer has gone all out with the decorations. There is tinsel and fake snow everywhere, even though Christmas is still three weeks away.

"Spiked eggnog." Isabel pulls out a glass bottle of rum from her handbag. "I wanted to give it a little kick."

"They have alcohol here, you know." I giggle as she pours more of the brown liquid into my red cup.

"Not ten years old from Jamaica." She swigs it from the bottle and puts it back into her handbag. "It's been a long week for both of us. We need to have some fun." Isabel loves everything about Jamaica. Even though you can't tell it from looking at her, she's an island girl. Her granddad grew up in Jamaica, and she spent every summer there from ages three to eighteen. You'd have thought she was related to Bob Marley himself, the way she went on about reggae music and being from the islands.

"Yes, we do." I nod and grab her hand. "Let's go dance on the dance floor."

"What dance floor?" She looks around at the crowd of still people, most of whom aren't even moving to the music. That's the thing about office parties. People just don't know how to get loose.

"We make the dance floor." I grab her hand and check to make sure my brother isn't in the vicinity. Sam won't want me dancing on the tables at his work party. In fact, he only invited me because he felt sorry for me. And because our parents made him. Even though he is thirty and I am twenty-four, he still abides by what our parents tell him to do. I am an adult, but to our parents, I am still the youngest and their little girl. And so when I called them to moan about losing my job, breaking my favorite heels, and being unlovable, they immediately got in touch with him to look after me.

Sam and I both live in New York, and it is a far cry from our upbringing in a small town on the southwest coast of Florida. Our parents still live in the Sunshine State and are constantly worried about us, especially me, living in the big city.

"Ella, I am not drunk enough to be Coyote Ugly right now." Isabel shakes her head, but she still raises her arm up in the air in her signature dance move, and I grin. Isabel and I are always the life of the party. In fact, that's how we met—at a freshman party during our first week of college. We were both standing in a corner, staring at cute guys and doing the Macarena when the song played, even though everyone else was acting like they were too cool. We hadn't ended up meeting any guys, but that had been the beginning of a fast and immediate friendship. We were both a little guy crazy back then (some may say we still are), but neither one of us had actually been in a super-serious relationship.

"Is the hot guy still looking at me?" I ask and look around before she can answer. I'm disappointed to see he is not in my line of sight any longer. "Maybe he wasn't even looking at me," I say to Isabel as I pull my black miniskirt down slightly. It's been riding up my thighs since I started swaying back and forth.

"Oh, he was looking." She giggles as she looks me up and down. I spin around and put on a little show for her. The alcohol is already going to my head. I can feel that it's going to be a good night. "You are dressed to kill." She fans herself, and I beam at her.

"So are you, darling." I point at her. We're both dressed up. We'd decided that tonight, we were going to look our sexiest. Not because we were trying to impress anyone but because we felt like we wanted to. I am wearing a short black miniskirt, with thigh-high boots that have a slight heel. My white top exposes part of my midriff when I dance, and the huge *V* between my boobs is not leaving much to the imagination. My hair hangs straight down my back, and my makeup is done to the nines. Not that anyone can tell due to the gold, glittery mask that is on my face. Isabel is wearing a short red dress with red heels, and she's curled her blonde hair so it bounces against her exposed shoulders. She looks like a blonde bombshell, and I am her brunette cousin. We look like a million dollars, and I want to ensure that we enjoy the night.

"Ella, there you are." My brother's deep voice sounds from next to me, and I give him my most innocent smile. I can see from his expression that he's not pleased with my attire, but then, he's always been a judgmental one. "What are you wearing?"

"Clothes." I roll my eyes. "How did you know it was me?" I ask him, wondering if I'm not as incognito as I thought.

"I heard you and Isabel laughing." He shakes his head as he looks over at my best friend. "You're both so loud."

"Thanks," I say in response, not letting him bother me. Sam can be a real bore sometimes. "Good to see you as well, big bro."

"Don't embarrass me, Ella." He frowns as he looks back at me, his black mask making him look more mysterious than it should. "This is a work event, and if you want me to try and get you a job here, then you need to be professional."

"Not interested, thanks." I grimace at his words. "I do not need your help. I think we both agree that your first try at helping me was a disaster." I don't add the part about how he helped me once before to get a job with his best friend, Colton Hart, and how I'd been fired one hour after starting said job for being unprofessional. I still haven't gotten over it. And I've certainly never forgiven Colton for what he did. In fact, I now consider him my nemesis and remind him of that every time that I see him. Which isn't often because I do my best to avoid him.

"Speaking of Colton..." Sam starts to bring up his friend, and I hold my hand up to stop him. I'm not interested in hearing anything about the man.

"Isabel and I are going to dance," I say, grabbing my friend's hand. "Let's get some more eggnog as well." I can see that Sam wants to say something else, but I don't care. When it comes to Colton, I no longer want to know. I spent far too many of my younger years thinking about him.

"Okay." She nods as we leave my brother standing there. She looks back at him wistfully, and I ignore it. I think, though I'm too scared to ask, that Isabel has a crush on Sam, but I don't really want to know. I do not want her to end up with him, as I know he's the biggest player on this side of Central Park. Along with his best friend and former roommate, Colton. They date so many women that they're lucky their dicks haven't fallen off yet.

Technically, I'm unsure if they are sleeping with all the women they take on dates, but I'm sure the number is more than zero. Not that I am going to ask.

"See anyone you like?" I ask and point to a group of guys that are standing next to the food table. I know it's a stupid question because we can't actually see anyone, but I need to get her mind off my brother.

"I can't tell what anyone looks like," she says as we make our way to the eggnog table. She pours more of the creamy goodness into our cups before grabbing her rum bottle and filling our glasses with the potent brown liquor. "After this, we do tequila shots," she adds as we click our plastic cups together in cheers. I sip on the beverage this time; the spiked eggnog has already given me a small buzz.

I can feel eyes on me, and I look around furtively to see who's watching me. It's the pin-striped guy again. I grin to myself as I deliberately keep my eyes moving, even though I can see him staring at me. It feels thrilling to have someone paying such close attention to me. I down the rest of my drink and start jumping up and down when the low-budget DJ of the party changes the song to Lil John and The Eastside Boyz.

"Let's get low, baby." I squeal as Isabel starts dancing as well. I grab her hand, and we start dancing. I can see that we're attracting a lot of attention now. I guess it's not every day that two hot girls start busting a move in the middle of a prim-and-proper law firm party. I spin around as Isabel lowers her ass to the floor and jumps up again. I'm happy to see that some other people are now bobbing their heads in time to the music.

I look over to see if my admirer is still staring at me, and he is. His mask is completely covering his face, but I can see he has generous lips. I'm not sure what comes over me, but I dance toward him, strutting my stuff before stopping a few feet away from him, spinning around, and twerking my ass back at him. I spin around again and lick my index finger, and point at him as I continue dancing my ass off. Isabel comes dancing over to me, and she and I dance for a few more minutes before the lights get dimmer and the music changes to Eminem.

There are several people who join us on the makeshift dance floor in the middle of the room now, and I'm laughing as I watch two geeky-looking guys do the robot. Someone hands me a shot glass, and I down it, feeling young, sexy, and happy. I can see that Isabel is also enjoying herself as we dance. A guy grabs her hand and spins her around, and they start dancing. I smile and continue dancing.

Then I feel a pair of strong, warm arms wrap around my waist, and someone starts dancing behind me. He's tall and muscular, and I'm about to push him away when I see his jacket sleeve. It's Pin-Striped Suit. I smile to myself as we dance. He's got rhythm, and he smells good. I feel his hands moving up and down on my waist, and I know I should slap them away, but I don't. I'm starting to feel turned on.

We're dancing closer and faster now. I can feel him behind me, and I back my ass up slightly as we dance. He seems to like the teasing because his fingers move up and down, testing their limits now. When I feel his hands brush up against my breasts, I pause slightly. Then they move back against my waist, and we continue dancing. Someone decides to lower the lights even more, and more people join us. We're now pushed against other people who are taking advantage of the dark to get frisky. His hands lift my top up slightly, and I feel his palms against my bare stomach; his fingers are silky and warm, and I don't hate the way he's making me feel.

I close my eyes, enjoying the moment. When he grabs my hips and brings me back toward him, I don't resist, even when I feel a hardness pressed up against my ass. Fuck! I giggle to myself as I feel him grinding up against me. I should be flustered that this stranger is turned on and letting me feel his hardness, but I'm not. In fact, I'm turned on. He seems to realize this because his fingers are moving upward again. And this time, it's not a casual brush against my underboob; his fingers move all the way up, and as they come down, he flicks my nipples. My panties are immediately wet. I cannot believe what I'm doing, though I know I'm not going to stop. This is the hottest night I've had in years.

We continue dancing, him letting me know just how turned on he is as he grinds against my ass. His palms cup my breasts as we dance, and when he moves them back down, I'm disappointed. Then I feel his fingers lifting my shirt up slightly, and then his fingers are under the material. I bite down on my lip as I feel him pinching my nipples. I'm close to coming, and I can't believe what I'm doing. He shifts slightly, and I feel him guiding me to the side of the room. I'm not sure what his plan is, but I'm not about to stop him.

Suddenly, we're next to the wall. I'm about to spin around so I can look into his eyes and possibly take his mask off, but he presses my hands up against the wall and pushes me forward slightly. He then dry humps me from behind as we continue dancing. This man knows how to work his hips as he rubs against me in time to the music. He pulls me back up, and I feel his arms around my waist again, only this time, his fingers slide down into my skirt instead of up. I gasp as they move deftly down into my panties. I hear his gasp as he feels how wet I am. I groan as he rubs my clit.

"Fuck." He grunts into my ear. It's the first word he's said to me, and it's hot. His voice is husky and tinged with lust.

"Is that what you want to do?" I giggle slightly as I pull his hand out of my panties regretfully. As much as I want this to go further, I cannot risk my brother catching me at his work party. He would kill me. I shift my body so I can spin around. He pins me against the wall as he moves in closer to me.

"Yes." He grunts as he lifts his fingers up and sticks them in his mouth. It is one of the sexiest things I've ever seen, and I can feel my heart racing. I have no idea where Isabel is, but I know she's going to freak out when I tell her about my night. I'm about to ask if I can pull his mask off when his mouth crashes down on mine. He tastes like whiskey, and his body is hard and controlled as he pulls me into him.

His hands squeeze my ass as his tongue enters my mouth, and I kiss him back eagerly as I wrap my arms around his neck. It's a little awkward with the masks on, but it still works. His right hand moves up and down the side of my body, and I feel like my body is about to explode as we stand there making out. This is exactly what I needed. I reach my hand down and rub the front of his pants. He's hard, and from what I can tell, he's long and thick. That only makes me more excited.

"Fuck yeah." He growls against my lips as I squeeze his cock gently. He grabs my hand and guides me out of the room toward the emergency exit. We both know what we want, and I only hope that he has protection on him. He pulls me out of the room and into the alley and lifts me up, his hands squeezing my ass as I wrap my legs around his waist. He leans in for a kiss, and I blink rapidly, trying to adjust to the sudden light as he kisses me again. My breasts are pressed up against his chest, and his right hand is pulling my hair as we kiss. He shifts slightly, and I feel his fingers between my legs again, moving my panties to the side.

"Oh," I gasp as cool air hits me there. I look at his face, and my heart thuds as his blue eyes stare at me from behind the mask. Familiar blue eyes. My heart lurches as panic hits my brain. His fingers are rubbing my clit urgently, and I'm moaning as I suddenly realize who I'm with.

"Colton," I gasp as reality takes hold of me. I reach forward and pull his mask up. His handsome, cocky face is staring at me, the unmistakable glint in his eyes making me shudder. "Oh, hell no."

"What?" He laughs, pulling my mask off. "Ella?" He looks just as shocked as I am as we stand there. His finger is still idly rubbing my clit as we stare at each other, and I can feel my legs trembling.

"Put me down." I clamber for some decorum. I cannot believe I've been making out with my archnemesis. The man of my nightmares. The one and only Colton Hart, the jackass of all jackasses. He lowers me to the ground gently, and we just stand there for a few seconds. He cocks his head to the side and then slowly reaches over to me and pulls my skirt down. I watch as he sucks his fingers again. There's a glint in his eyes as he leans forward and whispers in my ear, "We can go back to my place and have a one-night truce." He blows in my ear as he speaks, and I can barely concentrate. My body is still turned on, even though I'm beside myself. He looks into my eyes. "You know that you want—"

"What I want is for you to just shut up." I glare at him, annoyed by the cocky look on his handsome face. How had I not known he was going to be at the party? Was that what Sam had been about to tell me?

"That can be arranged." He grins wickedly.

"What?"

"You can shut me up by sitting on my face." He wraps his arm around my waist and pulls me into him so I can feel his hardness against my stomach. "Don't you want to come, Ella?" He presses his lips against my neck, and all I can think is, *Yes, yes, yes.* I don't even care that it's him. Right now, all I need is a sweet release.

"Just shut up and let's go," I say quickly, not wanting to think about it too much. He growls and drags me to the main road and signals a cab. We get into the back seat, and before I can even think about changing my mind, he's pulling me onto his lap and playing with my breasts as we kiss. I know the taxi driver is probably getting a view because Colton yanks my top up as we speed down the road, playing with my naked breasts and pinching my nipples, and I don't even care. I'm close to coming in the back of the taxi. And I know he is as well because I've positioned myself on his erection and am grinding back and forth on him like I'm a stripper hoping to make a big tip.

When the taxi arrives at his apartment, we stumble out. I'm wetter than I've ever been in my life. We enter the apartment, and he carries me into his room like I'm his newlywed bride. He lowers me onto the bed, and as I stare up at him, all I can think is that it doesn't surprise me that he's so cocky and sure of himself. This is the hottest night of my life. Before I know what's happening, he's pulling my panties down and rolling me onto him. He lifts me up, and I scoot forward. I know what he wants me to do. My skirt is bunched around my waist, and I cry out as I lower myself onto his face. His tongue is ready for me, and his arms rock me back and forth against his lips and nose as he eats me out. I scream as his tongue enters me, and I feel myself coming on his face harder than I've ever come on another guy's dick.

He pushes me to the side, and I watch as he pulls all of

his clothes off and then pulls the rest of my clothes off as well. He's tender and dominant, and I don't even have time to think as he rolls the condom onto his hardness and positions himself between my legs. He kisses me hard as he thrusts into me, and I cry out as he starts fucking me. I feel like I'm on another planet as he pleasures me. I can hear myself screaming as he thrusts harder and faster.

"Scream for me, Ella." He growls. "I know you've been dreaming about this big cock for years." He grunts as he pulls my legs above his shoulders. My jaw drops at his words, but I can't even process a response because I can barely think. My body is so possessed by his actions that I'm not even mad at the satisfied look on his face as he reaches down to rub my clit and continues thrusting inside of me. My entire body shakes as I come again, and then he freezes suddenly and pulls out of me. I watch as he pulls the condom off, and he spurts his hot cum all over my stomach and breasts, some even landing on my chin. He chuckles as I stare up at him in shock.

"Your dreams came true tonight, Ella." He winks at me. "Aren't you a lucky woman?"

All I can do is stare at him. My brain is still trying to process what has just happened. I just had sex with Colton Hart. My brother's best friend. My nemesis. My old boss. I can't believe it. He's still full of himself, and just a few moments ago, I was full of him. I wasn't sure how I was going to live this down. I yawn, suddenly realizing I'm tired. I need to leave, but I also need to sleep. Colton lies down next to me, and we just stare at each other. I suddenly realize the enormity of what we've just done. Shit! I groan to myself. How have I let this happen?

2

Dear Diary,
 Colton Hart, my brother's best friend, is the most obnoxious, most annoying person I've ever met. I literally can't stand him. Once upon a time, he was my boss, and he fired me after one hour!
 Yes, one hour!
 Just because he's hot and rich, he thinks he runs the world.
 Well, guess what, Colton?
 You don't run me!
 I mean, okay, maybe last night, you kinda had me. But that was a mistake. A huge mistake. Pun intended because we both know it wasn't that huge.
 Am I still blushing?
 No!
 NO!
 Okay, maybe a little, but I have bigger problems now. Way bigger.
 Ella
 XOXO

I wake up and immediately know that something isn't

right. I open my eyes slowly and then freeze as I look over and see that Colton is lying next to me. All of a sudden, the memories of the previous evening come flashing back into my mind. How I'd gone to Sam's Christmas party, how Isabel had spiked the eggnog, how I'd started dancing and she told me that a good-looking guy was staring at me. I cringe as I think about the way I danced and waved my hands in front of him and the way his fingers slid up my body and squeezed my breasts, and now, here I was.

"Morning, sunshine." His deep voice is husky, and I notice that his eyes are open and staring at me. There's a twinkle in his eyes that I know he is giving me on purpose.

"Not a good morning," I say, sitting up. The sheet falls down and exposes my naked breasts, and I grab it quickly.

"Nothing I haven't already seen now." He winks, and I glare at him.

"Last night was a mistake," I say quickly. "If you're a gentleman, you will close your eyes so that I can get out of this bed and put on my clothes and—"

"What, you don't want seconds?" He leans forward and reaches up to kiss me.

I push him away. "What do you think you're doing?"

"You weren't saying no to my kisses last night."

"That's because I—"

"And you can't pretend you didn't know it was me. In fact, I think you did it on purpose."

"Did what on purpose?" I stare at him, blinking rapidly.

"You teased me so I would come over to you because this is what you've wanted all along." His eyes are wide, and he looks down at his body. "And now you've had me, all eight inches of me."

My jaw drops. "You did not just say that."

"True," he says, tilting his head to the side. "It could be eight and a half. I haven't measured in a long while."

"Colton Hart, this is not an appropriate conversation to be having with me."

"Why not?" he says, raising a single eyebrow. He bites down on his lip and runs his fingers through his golden-brown hair.

I try not to stare at his fingers too hard because they are reminding me of what they were doing to me on the dance floor and in his bed the previous evening. Why, oh why, was I so stupid as to agree to a night with him? What had I been thinking? "You weren't thinking," I muttered under my breath. I had been thinking with one body part and one body part alone.

"What are you saying?" he asks, gazing at me. There's a chuckle in his voice now, and I know he thinks it's absolutely hilarious.

"I'm saying that last night was not something I would have thought I'd do in a million years."

"But you hoped to, didn't you?"

"No, I did not." My hands are on my hips now. I jump out of the bed, holding the sheet to me. That is a mistake. I look down at his naked body lying there. His cock is at attention. "You're hard?!" The words are out of my mouth before I can stop them. I blush as he winks again. He runs his right hand down to his cock and holds it in his hand.

"What, you've never heard of morning wood?" he says, glancing at me and smiling. "And up until about two minutes ago, you were pressed up against my cock and I was thinking that we'd have a morning quickie and—"

"Oh my gosh, please stop. This is not happening. Oh my gosh." I close my eyes and count to three. "One, two, three." I open them hoping I'm gonna be in my bed and waking from a dream, but I just see his cocky face staring back at me. I can't believe it. I slept with Colton Hart, my brother's best friend, my archnemesis, the man who fired me after one hour of working for him, and the same man who told everyone that I was unprofessional when I hadn't done anything unprofessional. He was just a jackass. I couldn't stand him, and yet I slept with him because... I didn't even know why. Sure, I'd been horny, and sure, he'd had the moves, but as soon as I'd seen his face, his twinkling, familiar, blue eyes, I should have said no. I should have gone back into the law firm and found some geeky lawyer to dance with and then just gone home.

"Considering it?" he says, looking at his Rolex because, of course, he would have a Rolex—he's Colton Hart.

"I'm not considering anything. I need to leave right now, and we are never going to talk about this. In fact, I don't want to see you—again."

"You do realize your brother is my best friend?"

"He may be your best friend, but that doesn't mean we have to hang out."

"But your parents invited me over for Christmas lunch."

"Well, then, we don't have to see each other for three weeks," I say, counting on my fingers. "We have three weeks until Christmas. And then at Christmas, we'll pretend that we haven't seen each other in years. Then we'll have lunch and we'll leave and forget this ever happened."

"Okay, but if you want, we can have one last moment of fun for you to remember and fantasize about."

"Ewww! Are you absolutely out of your mind?"

"No, but you have ten minutes to get ready before your brother arrives."

"What?!" I scream. "What are you talking about? You don't live with Sam anymore. You guys have your own places."

"Yeah, but he's coming over this morning. I thought you would've known that."

"Why would I know that?" I say. "I don't keep track of your schedule, and I certainly don't keep track of Sam's schedule."

"So is that a yes or a no?" He jumps up and walks over to me. His blue eyes have a devious glint in them as he leans down and kisses me on the lips.

I don't know what to do. My body tingles as I stare at him. I place my palms against his shoulders to push him away, but instead, they somehow seem to wrap around his neck. "We're not doing this," I say, glaring at him.

He laughs, moving his hands so he can squeeze my naked ass. "Last night was good though, huh?" he whispers in my ear, and for a few seconds, I remember what it felt like to feel him thrusting inside of me. I blink and pull away.

"No, this is not gonna happen." I push him away and quickly grab my clothes. I'm pulling on my skirt and then my top when I realize that I forgot to put on my panties. I grab them from the floor and discover I'm also holding his boxers. "You can—" I freeze as I hear the front door slam. "What is going on?" I say, my face going red. Footsteps are heading toward the door.

"Hey, you up yet?" It's my brother's voice, and I stare at Colton, who is laughing. *Fuck! What am I going to do?* I think.

3

There is something about fear that will stop you in your tracks, even though you know that this is the moment that you should be moving faster than you've ever moved before. I can hear Sam's voice on the other side of the door, and my heart feels like it is going to fall out of my body. Like I am going to pass out. "Respond to him!" I hiss at Colton. He is trying not to laugh. He runs his fingers through his hair again and shakes his head.

"Why don't you say something before he opens the door? What are you thinking?" I hit him. "Do you want him to kill me and you?"

"I don't know," he says. "Do you?"

"What did you say?" Sam bangs on the door. "I can't hear you. You decent? Can I come in?"

"Hold on, dude," Colton says. "I'm just finishing up some work here."

"Oh, this early?"

Colton chuckles. "You know me, always working."

I glare at him for a couple of seconds. "What am I going to do?" I say, more to myself than to him because I know he's not going to be a help in this situation. He thinks it's funny, even though he knows my brother would annihilate him if he knew what Colton had done to me the previous evening.

"What's it gonna be?" he says. "You could hide in my closet or under my bed, or—"

"I'm not hiding under your bed."

"You can hide in the bed," he says. "I'll go and play basketball with your brother. I'll be back in about an hour. Then I'll take a shower and you can scrub me, clean me up." He licks his lips, his fingers reach over to my stomach, and he runs them down to my belly button. "And then I can clean you up," he says, grinning. "I seem to remember that your stomach got a little sticky last night."

Oh my gosh, this is not happening, I think, blinking fast. *Think, think, think, Ella. You need to use your brain right now.* I know I look absolutely crazy, but I don't know what else to do.

"Dude, what's going on?" Sam says.

Colton grins and then points to his bed. "You want to get under it or in it?"

"Neither," I say. "You are so lucky that I don't have a—"

"Hey, you can come in." Colton chuckles, and Sam tries the door. I nearly fall on the ground, but that's when I realize it's locked.

Thank you, dear Jesus. Someone is looking out for me, I think. I watch as Colton walks into the bathroom, wraps a towel around his waist and heads over to the door. "What are you doing?" I say. He looks back at me and shrugs, and I just stand there like a fool.

"Hey, sorry about that, Sam."

"No worries." My brother pauses as he looks into the room and sees me standing there. "Ella!" He frowns slightly and steps inside. He looks at me, then he looks at Colton, and then he looks at me again. "What's going on?" he asks. He doesn't sound like he's happy, and I know that he will kill me, and then he'll tell my parents and they'll kill me as well.

And then, for the fun of it, I'll just kill myself because I am the idiot who slept with Colton Hart.

"So there's something I have to tell you," Colton says to Sam, and I step forward.

"Yeah," Sam says. He's growling now, and looks pissed. "What is going on?" I am wondering what he knows about last night.

"I am Colton's new assistant," I say quickly. "He said he would give me another chance because he felt bad about firing me so quickly last time." I'm not sure where the words are coming from, but they are coming. Colton looks amused, and my brother looks like he doesn't really believe what I'm saying. "And I got here really early because I wanted to prove to him that I'm gonna be really responsible this time, so I'm even doing his laundry." I hold up Colton's boxers in my hand. I want to sink into the ground. I feel stupid. I feel—

"Wow! Colton, man, I really appreciate that." Sam puts his arms around Colton's shoulders. "I know she messed up last time. I know she just got fired again, and she really needs it." My jaw drops.

My brother doesn't actually believe this, does he? And now he's thanking Colton for giving me a job after firing me and saying I am the reason why I keep getting fired when it totally was not my fault. "My boss was having an affair, and he thought I was a private detective working for his wife," I remind Sam, glaring at him. "That's why."

"Sure, Ella," he says, looking at me. "You're still wearing last night's clothes because why? You forgot to change before coming over this morning? Or were you just out partying all night and then realized you had to be at work early this morning, so you just showed up like that? So unprofessional. If Mom and Dad knew—"

I stare at him, my jaw slack.

This is not happening. I almost don't know whether or not I should correct him. I can tell him that the reason I am wearing last night's clothes is because I spent the night here and didn't have a change of clothes, but I have a feeling that his reaction will be a whole lot worse. "Yep, you got me," I say. "So Colton, or should I call you Mr. Hart?"

"You can call me sir if you want," he says in response, and I just shake my head.

"Colton, is there any other laundry that you want me to do for you?"

"Well, I was just about to get it together for you, so can you give me a couple of minutes?"

"Of course, sir," I say in my most cheery voice. I know I sound like a bitch, but I just can't believe I am having to make up this story.

Sam is beaming now. "This is so cool. Mom and Dad were so worried about you. They had even asked me to see if I could get you a job at the firm and lend you some money, but now you don't need it because you got a job with Colton, and I know you're not gonna screw this one up, right?"

"What?" I blink at him.

"We're all flying to Florida in a few weeks, and I know Mom and Dad will want to hear all about the job. It's gonna look really bad if Colton has to fire you again right before Christmas."

"Well, maybe I'll get another job that pays a little bit better," I say. "Colton knows that this is just temporary until —"

"Hey, Ella," he says, "I decided that I'm gonna meet your salary requirements because I know you're gonna do a much better job than you did last time. I mean, you already got here so early and decided that you wanted to help clean up."

"Clean up?" I stare at him.

"My apartment, right?"

"You said you were gonna do laundry and clean up the apartment because my housekeeper quit last week and I haven't been able to find anyone yet. I have a date tonight, so it has to look good."

"You have a date tonight?" I blink at him. Was he really this much of a pig?

"Yeah," he says, "so I'm going to need this place real clean. You get what I'm saying?" I stare at him, and he stares at me, and all I want to do is scream.

4

I stand there feeling quite dumbfounded at what just happened. Before I can even say anything else, Colton pulls on a pair of basketball shorts and a T-shirt.

"So I'm off now. Do you think you'll be able to take care of everything while I'm playing basketball with Sam?" Colton looks at me in the way that he does. That annoys me the most. He thinks just because he's six years older than me and a successful businessman that he's the boss of me. And just because I'm pretending he is the boss of me doesn't mean that I like it.

"Yes, sir. Of course," I say in my sweetest, most courteous voice.

He grins. "I like that. You've really matured, Ella," he says, giving me a slap on the shoulder as if we're buddies.

"Well, I would love to say the same thing about you, but..." My voice trails off as I see Sam giving me a sly look. I know he's wondering why I'm talking to Colton that way. Sometimes, Sam acts like he's my dad instead of my older brother. I suppose it is because of the age gap and the fact that he always had to look out for me when we were younger. But he has to realize that I am no longer a kid. I am twenty-four years old now and granted, though I don't have a job and it doesn't look like I am getting another one anytime soon, I can still take care of myself. I really can.

"So I'll leave you here to get everything ready and to do my laundry." Colton smiles, and I watch as he and Sam walk out the door.

"He doesn't really think I'm going to do his laundry, does he?" I mumble to myself as I stand there. I'm not quite sure what to do. I grab my phone so I can call Isabel because I am literally flabbergasted. She picks up the phone almost immediately.

"Hey there. What happened to you last night?" she asks, and I let out a loud groan. "Oh boy. I'm sitting down. Tell me what happened."

"You'll not believe where I am right now," I say, sitting on the edge of Colton's bed.

"Please do not tell me you're in jail. We do not have bail money."

"No, I'm not in jail. Why would you think I'm in jail? Come on, Isabel."

"I don't know, but you were dancing up a storm, and I saw you dancing with that guy. I didn't know if you were going to get arrested for public..." She pauses and giggles.

"Public what?" I growl.

"You know."

"What are you saying?"

"Public intoxication," she says innocently.

"Is that what you were really thinking?"

"No, that's not what I was thinking. Public sex. You were all over that guy."

"I was not all over that guy. He was all over me and—"

"Girl, you were both all over each other. I saw you guys bumping and grinding on the dance floor, and it looked like it was getting really intimate. And I was just thinking to myself, *Wow, I did not think that my best friend, Ella, could do all that with a stranger.*"

"Turns out he wasn't a stranger." I moan, not knowing how I'm ever gonna live this down.

"What do you mean he wasn't a stranger? Oh my gosh. Was he someone famous?" She's excited now. "Like Hugh Jackman?"

"What?!" I screech into the phone. "What are you talking about? Why would Hugh Jackman be on the dance floor making out with me?"

"I don't know. Who was it, then?"

"No one good."

"What do you mean no one good? You looked like you were enjoying it."

"Okay. I was enjoying it, but that was until I knew who it was."

"Oh my gosh. Who was it? Tell me, tell me!" she squeals.

"It was Colton."

"Colton?" she says.

"Yes!" I interrupt her. "Colton Hart, my brother's best friend. The guy that fired me when I was eighteen years old after working for him for one hour. That jackass."

"Oh boy. So what happened? You guys were making out and then you saw it was him and you slapped him and went and got a hotel room because you were too ashamed or something?"

"No, that's not what happened."

"Then tell me, what happened? You ran away and you ended up in—"

"I went back home with him."

There is silence on the other side of the phone. "You what? No way."

"Way. It's your fault, Isabel."

"How is it my fault?"

"Because you spiked the eggnog."

"Yeah, because you were the one that was going on and on about how we needed to have fun and let loose, and you wanted to get drunk because you hadn't gotten drunk in so long. Remember, that's exactly what you said. And you wanted us to have the time of our lives. And—"

"I know what I said, but I didn't expect the alcohol to go to my head like that."

"Oh, so you were so drunk that you didn't even realize it was him?"

"No, I knew it was him."

"So then?"

"So by the time I realized it was him, I was so turned on and horny I couldn't say no. And well, you know, he's good-looking."

"He is good-looking," she says, with a dreamy expression on her face. "Those blue eyes of his."

"I know, they are just mesmerizing. Don't tell him I said that, though." I wrinkle my nose because I hate the fact that I find him so handsome. If I thought he looked like a donkey's ass, then I wouldn't be in any of the trouble I was currently in.

"Of course I would never tell him you said that. So when you say you guys hooked up, are we talking first base or…?"

"Really, Isabel? Are we in eighth grade?"

"What? I'm just asking."

❋

"Hey there, dancing queen." Isabel's voice carries loudly down the street as I approach her. She's standing outside the café with a cup of coffee in her hand, and I feel like I'm doing the walk of shame as I make my way over to her. "Still in your miniskirt, I see."

"I didn't exactly have time to change." I run my fingers

through my long, dark, messy hair and try to tame it before we enter the coffee shop. "I'm so embarrassed. How am I going to look Colton in the face the next time I see him?"

"Well, you don't have to look him in the face." She pauses and then starts giggling. I stare at her for a few seconds, wondering if she's still drunk from last night. It was my idea to dance the night away, but she certainly joined in.

"You okay?" I ask as she leans forward, her blue eyes wide with mirth.

"You don't have to look him in the face if you don't want to," she says again. "You can sit on it instead."

"Isabel." I hit her in the shoulder and glance around quickly to ensure no one heard her. "Really?"

"Too soon?" She giggles again. "And was that something Colton said last night?"

"Was what something Colton said last night?" I repeat stupidly, and then it hits me what she's referring to. "No, he's not a five-minute man if that's what you're asking." I grin and blush at the same time as I think about the previous evening. There are many reasons why Colton Hart gets on my nerves, but his lovemaking is not one of them.

"I take it that he left you satisfied, then." She holds open the door to the café and we walk inside and grab a booth. "Your dry spell is finally done."

"I just wish it hadn't been with him." I groan and bury my face in my hands. What was I thinking? He will never let me live this down. He tasted me. He was inside of me. He heard me screaming his name. "I can't believe I had a one-night stand. And how can I have been so desperate as to sleep with Colton?"

"I still don't understand. At what point did you realize it was him?" she asks as she opens her menu. I look down at my menu as well, though I'm almost sure I know what I want. I'm a creature of habit. I almost always have French toast with bacon or a cheese and ham omelet with breakfast potatoes.

"You want to share something sweet with me?" Isabel grins. "And then we get our own savory dish?"

"I am hungry."

"You had a real workout last night." She leans back and tightens her hair band around her wispy, blonde hair. She rubs her eyes, and I can see the traces of eyeliner under her eyes. Looks like she hasn't been awake for that long, either. Isabel is normally a woman who takes off her makeup religiously each night.

"What do we look like?" I pick up a spoon and stare at my reflection. I look rougher than I thought. My no-smear mascara is smeared, and my eyeliner is smudged. My hair is frizzy at the front, and my cheeks are bright red.

"We look like two young women who had a fun night last night." She sips from her coffee cup. "Only you had a lot better time than I did."

"Maybe." I groan. "Anyway, I want to forget all about it. Hopefully, I will not see Colton again for the next ten years."

"Isn't he going home with you to Florida this year?" she reminds me as if the thought is not in the back of my mind.

"He's not going home with me," I say quickly. "My parents invited him because he's Sam's best friend and he has nowhere else to go now that his parents live in Europe." I sigh. "It would have been nice if they'd asked me if I minded."

"Well, they didn't," she points out matter-of-factly. "So you know you're going to see Mr. Lover Lover in—"

"Do not call him that." I close the menu and wait for the server to come and take our order. "I'm half wondering if someone didn't put a spell on me when I got to the firm yesterday."

"He dickmatized you."

"Well, I didn't have his dick until we left."

"Girl, I saw the way you were dancing with him. That man was grinding."

"Don't remind me." I blush. "I need to stop thinking about this." I'm about to start complaining about my poor judgment when my phone starts ringing. I look at the screen and see that it's Danny, a father I sometimes babysit for. His daughter, Frannie, is seven, and I've been taking care of her on and off for the last four years. Danny is a single father, his ex moved to Vegas to be with a male stripper she met and fell in love with at a bachelorette party. "It's Danny," I say as I answer the phone. "Hello, is everything okay?"

"Ella, good morning." Danny's voice is a bit nasal, and he sounds stressed. "I don't suppose you can come and look after Frannie this morning for a few hours?"

"I think so," I say. "I'm just having breakfast with Isabel right now, but when I'm done, I can come over."

"Perfect." He sounds relieved. "I have to go to Westchester to drop off some plants for a customer." He sighs. "She's spent a lot of money with me this year, and even though I don't normally offer delivery, she can't get to the city," he explains. Danny owns an exotic plant store that specializes in finding unique and expensive plants for rich customers across the state.

"No worries. I'll be there in about an hour."

"Perfect. Thanks so much, Ella. I don't know what we would do without you." He sounds much calmer now. "I will tell Frannie now. She will be so excited to see you."

"Well, like I said, I lost my job last week, so I have more free time if you need me," I say, letting him know I'm available to babysit whenever he needs me, as I need as much money as I can get right now. I live in a studio apartment, but the rent is still quite high, and I don't have much money in my bank account.

"Thanks, Ella. See you soon." He hangs up, and I can see that Isabel is grinning as I put the phone down on the table.

"What is it?" I ask her.

"I thought you got a new job with Colton?"

"That's not real." I wrinkle my nose and shudder. "I just said that so Sam didn't realize I'd just banged his best friend. There's no way Colton would ever want to hire me again, and there's no way I would ever want to work for him again after last time."

"We'll see." There's a knowing look on Isabel's face, and I'm not even going to ask her what she's thinking. I don't want to know. I don't want to talk about Colton anymore. I just want to shower. And think about what happened in the comfort of my own space. I sigh as I realize I have to go over to Danny's first. I don't have time to go home and change. I am going to have to do another walk of shame. When Sam invited me to his work party, all I hoped for was to win a gift card or a bracelet from Tiffany's. I didn't expect to have a one-night stand with my nemesis and nearly get caught by my brother.

5

"Frannie, do you want a snack?" I ask as I open the fridge and look at the various contents inside. Danny hasn't exactly outdone himself with the grocery shopping, and there aren't many options. I know that neither one of us wants to eat moldy grapes or wilted spinach. "Or are you ready for dinner?"

"Chocolate chip cookies?" she asks hopefully, and I hide a smile. She reminds me of myself when I was a child. If I'm honest, I am still a woman who has questionable tastes in eating habits. I am the sort of woman who will always eat dessert before my main meal. I like my sweets. My self-control is not always where it should be. Maybe that is why I made such a big mistake with Colton. Not that I want to think about that. Especially not while I am babysitting.

"No cookies." I laugh as I pull out a cucumber and some baby carrots. "How about some yummy—"

"Those aren't yummy." She walks up behind me and shakes her head. Her two pigtails shake from side to side. "I want cookies."

"We can have cookies after dinner," I say, wondering at what age kids realize that tantrums rarely work to their advantage. I wonder if I pull a tantrum on Colton if he will continue being a jackass to me. "Are you hungry? We can make burgers and a nice big salad, and then we can play a game." I open the freezer to take out the frozen burger patties. I know Danny always has burgers. If he has to choose another career, I won't be shocked if he chooses to be the Hamburglar.

"Can I see your phone?" Frannie asks, holding her small hand out. "I wanna play *Minecraft*."

"Oh, honey, I don't have that on my phone." My words sound wonky as I hastily pick my phone up from the countertop. I've just spent the last fifteen minutes scrolling on Instagram and staring at photos of my friends in Florida, who all seem to be living the most glamorous lives ever. The last photo I was looking at was of two of my high school frenemies, Mercedes and Pauline; they were wearing skinny bikinis on South Beach and posing with their rich husbands while drinking frozen margaritas. I'd commented, "Lucky bitches," on the photo with a laughing emoji to show I was joking. I don't want Frannie to see that. I don't need her asking her dad what a bitch is.

Looking at the photos made me feel a little bit sad about the trajectory of my own life. I don't like to compare my life to others, but staring at their photos does make me feel like a bit of a loser.

Maybe even a big loser. BIG.

The photos are like a slap in the face that reminds me of the fact that I have no boyfriend, no hope of a husband, no money, and no access to exclusive vacations and private beaches.

"I want pizza." Frannie pouts in that way that tells me she's tempted to throw a temper tantrum. I love her, but I know that she goes into spoiled toddler mode if she doesn't get her own way. Her dad likes to give her everything she wants because he feels guilty that she doesn't have a mom. I don't know exactly what happened, but I do know that there doesn't seem to be any other female presence in Frannie's life.

"Frannie..." I pause and give her my widest smile. "I have an idea."

"Yes?" she asks hopefully, her big eyes staring at me. I start to feel slightly guilty because I know my suggestion is not going to be what she wants to hear.

"So what if we have a—"

"I want pepperoni and pineapple on my pizza. I like pineapple on pizza," she says in her small voice, and I stare at her in surprise. She already seemed to have it in her head that I was going to say yes to the pizza.

"You like pineapple on your pizza?" I'm taken aback slightly. Who likes pineapple on their pizza? Especially what kids?

"Yes, and anchovies." She rubs her belly, and I just stare at her. I've already forgotten what I was going to say.

"I don't even..." My phone starts ringing then and I stare at the screen.

"You can take it," Frannie says, trying to peer at the screen. "Who is it? Is it Daddy?"

I glance at the screen and try not to groan. "Oh, it's no one important." It's Colton. I have no idea why he's calling me, and I certainly don't want to speak to him. Even though my stomach is flipping in knots.

"You should pick it up," she says innocently. "It's rude not to answer the phone when someone calls you. That's what Daddy says." She folds her arms like my grandma used to do, and I sigh. I really do not want to answer the phone.

"I guess I don't want to be rude," I say as I answer. "Hello?" I try to make my tone as unpleasant as possible, even though my heart is racing. I still can't quite get over what happened the night before. I don't want to think about it. I don't want to be reminded of Colton, and I certainly don't want to be reminded of my brother walking in on us in the bedroom with me standing there with Colton's boxers in my hands. I freeze as I think about what would have happened if he'd walked in while we were still in bed.

"Is that you, Ella?" Colton says in a deep voice that reminds me of Michael Bublé, and I wish that it didn't because it's turning me on.

"Um, who else would it be?" I retort and then look at Frannie's curious eyes. She is really too young to be this nosy, eavesdropping on other people's conversations.

"Where are you?" he asks, annoyed, and I frown slightly. What is with the attitude?

"What do you mean, where am I?"

"You need to get over to my apartment right now."

"What?"

"It's important, and I need you here now."

"Can't happen. I am currently babysitting and—"

"Babysitting who?" he cuts me off, and I roll my eyes.

"You don't know her, and it's none of your business anyway."

"This is important. Get over here now. I mean it." He hangs up the phone before I can respond, and I want to scream. I want to call him back and tell him off for being so rude and snappy. Who does he think he is talking to me like that? I am about to call him back when I see Frannie stepping toward me.

"Is everything okay?" she asks me, batting her eyelashes. Is she trying to be a child star or what?

"Yeah, it's fine." I sigh. "You know what? Let's order this pizza."

"Yay! Yay!" She jumps up and down, the excitement on her face making me feel guilty for not immediately ordering the pizza. "I love you!"

"And I love you, too," I say, hugging her. "You are the sweetest little girl."

"I know. My daddy says that to me all the time. I'm the sweetest girl in all of New York City and possibly all of New Jersey as well."

"What?" I blink at her, surprised at how specific she's being.

"That's what Daddy says." She dances around. "But when I'm naughty, I'm only the third sweetest."

"Okay." I frown slightly, but I don't say anything. Who am I to question Danny's parenting techniques? Then I hear the front door opening, and I freeze. My heart races as I push the little girl behind me. "Oh my gosh. Stay back, Frannie." I grab her hand and frantically look around for something to use as a weapon. I grab a rolling pin and head toward the front door. Is someone breaking in?

"Who is it?" I shout in my most menacing voice.

"Hey, it's just me," Danny says as he walks toward us, a lopsided grin on his face. "Sorry to scare you guys."

"Oh, you're back already?" I stare at him in surprise. "I thought you had to go to Westchester. I thought you'd be gone hours."

"Turns out that the plan was not what I thought it was." He stares at me for a couple of seconds and shrugs. "So I figured I'd spend some time with my two best gals." His two best gals? I'm not sure what he means by that, and I'm not sure I want to ask him, either.

"Oh. Funny," I respond, figuring he is joking. I am pretty sure he only made the comment to make Frannie feel good and so that I wouldn't feel bad. I don't want to tell him that I won't be offended if he doesn't include me. I am only the babysitter, after all.

"I love you, Daddy." Frannie runs toward him, and he picks her up and spins her around. "We were just going to get pizza. Pepperoni and pineapple. Do you want to get one as well?"

"I hope you don't mind," I say quickly, hoping he's not

going to be mad that I'm not cooking something. "She really wanted pizza, and..."

"I love pizza." He grins as he puts Frannie back down on the ground. He takes a step toward me and winks. "Sounds great to me. And you're okay with pineapple and pepperoni?"

"Not my favorite," I admit with a laugh, then hear my phone beep. I bet it's Colton demanding something from me. I want to ignore him, but I have to admit I am intrigued as to what he wants. "Actually, seeing as you're back, I might leave now instead. Is that okay?"

"Oh." There's a look of disappointment on his face, which surprises me. "Hmm, I was kind of hoping to do some work, but if you really have to go..."

"I mean, if you have to work," I say quickly, "of course I'll stay." I don't want him to think that I'm shirking my responsibilities, especially not for Colton.

"I mean, it's okay if you have something you need to do."

"My new boss called and said he needs to see me," I explain, feeling guilty about the half-truth.

"She did get a phone call, and I think she has to go, Daddy."

"Yeah. It was kind of from my new boss-ish," I say again, not sure why I brought Colton up in that way, since he isn't really my boss. Or anyone I really want to go rush and see.

"Oh, you got a job already. Congratulations." He smiles, but he doesn't seem super happy. "I'd been hoping we'd see you around here a bit more often."

"Um, it's kind of a job and kind of not, but..." I blush slightly. No way I want to get into this conversation with him. Even if Frannie hadn't been there. What a mess. "But he did say he needs to see me about something."

"Sure, Ella. If your boss is calling, you should go. Maybe next time we can have dinner." He stares at me, and I just nod, not really sure what he's saying. Maybe next time we can have dinner? Why would we have dinner if I am babysitting Frannie?

"Thank you. Bye, Frannie." I lean over and give her a big hug. "See you soon?"

"Bye," she says in her soft, sweet voice. I look over at Danny, and he embraces me in a big, warm hug.

"Thank you for always being here for us. You really are one in a million." He rubs my back, and I just stand there slightly awkwardly. Is he pressing me into him, or am I imagining it?

"Oh, thank you." I stand there holding him, feeling slightly weird that the hug is still continuing after twenty seconds. He's still rubbing my back, but then he steps back.

"You really are the backbone of this family."

"I am?" I stare at him, feeling slightly confused at his words. Am I really as good as Mary Poppins? Somehow, I doubt she'd have ordered a pizza.

"I mean, you're always here for Frannie when I need you," he says. "That means a lot to me."

"You're welcome. Anytime." I grab my belongings quickly and head to the front door. "Bye, guys. Enjoy your pizza. I'll see you later." I leave before he can say anything else and try not to ponder upon his words too long. Danny has always been an interesting character. I guess he really is grateful for all my help. I've heard it is hard to find good nannies in the city.

❋

I arrive at Colton's about thirty-five minutes later, and my heart is racing. I hate that I rushed over here, but I also hate not knowing what's going on. My anxiety can't stand being in the dark. I need to find out why he wanted me over here so quickly. I take a deep breath as I enter the building and then the elevator. I brush my fingers through my hair as I make my way out of the elevator and head to his door. I ring the doorbell and wait. My heart leaps as he opens the door. He blinks at me and frowns before moving aside.

"Inside," he says, growling. I step into the apartment, wondering what this is about. Has my brother found something out? Is he mad at Colton? Is Colton blaming me for the lie? I bite down on my lip and stare at him.

"What's going on?" I ask him. "I don't even get a hello?"

"You didn't tidy up." He frowns and gestures to the kitchen.

I blink at him in confusion for a couple of seconds and look around the apartment.

"Sorry, what?" I'm not sure if I've misunderstood him or if he's losing his mind.

"I said you haven't tidied up my apartment. The bed isn't made. The dishes aren't done. I thought you would've vacuumed." My jaw drops as he pauses and tuts.

"What?" I gaze at him. "You're not being serious right now, are you?" I wait for him to laugh and say, "April Fools," because this has to be a joke.

"As my new assistant and housekeeper, I expect you to take your duties seriously." His lips thin, and he shakes his head. "Do I have to call Sam?"

"Dude, I'm not really your assistant. I don't work for you, okay? That was just something we made up so Sam didn't kill us both."

"No, Ella. I think we made it very clear that you are my new assistant."

"What?"

"And let's be real, you didn't last very long the first time. I would hate for you to get fired again so quickly. Your parents would be so disappointed...unless, of course, you just wanted the truth to come out."

"Are you out of your mind?" I cross my arms and stare at him. My eyes are shooting daggers at him. If I were a dragon and I could summon fire from my mouth, I would scorch him with the deadliest heat I could. My heart is racing. Sam would kill me if he knew I slept with his best friend. My parents would take an emergency trip to the Vatican to pray for me, thinking I was spiraling out of control. "You are a prick, Colton," I say distinctly. He smirks slightly and takes a step toward me. His blue eyes are shimmering as he looks down at my lips.

"I wouldn't say I am a prick, but I will admit that I do have a prick. A very big prick." He winks at me. "A big prick that you seem to like. Remember how you were going, 'Ooh, ah, give it to me,' all night long?" He grabs my hand, and I pull it away from him and start coughing. "Are you okay? Are you choking?" he asks in concern, and I blush.

"I'm fine. You are the most..." I pause as he runs his fingers through his hair and then undoes the top button of his shirt. What is he doing?

"What?" He grins and undoes another button. "I'm the most hung guy you've ever been with? I know that already, hun."

"Ugh. I cannot believe I slept with you. I must've been out of my mind. I was drunk. You know that's why it happened, right? If I'd known how annoying you'd be, I never would have given you a glance."

"Sure, if you *would've* known. We both know you knew who I was from the second you saw me standing on the dance floor, and you did everything in your power to seduce me and get me. And, well, you got lucky. Now here we are, and while I will admit that you know how to back that ass up, that's not going to exempt you from your responsibilities."

"Responsibilities?" I glare at him, even though I half want to laugh at his "back that ass up" comment. My voice rises. "I don't want this job, and I don't care what you have to say. If you think for one second that I am going to be cleaning up your apartment, then..." I pause as he undoes another button, and I stare at a large expanse of tanned, brown skin.

"What? Would you rather get some and then clean up?" he says, stepping toward me. He licks his lips slowly and deliberately. I can see his eyes on my chest. He reaches up and runs his hands through his silky blond hair again, his blue eyes twinkling as he gazes at me. It should be illegal to be that handsome and that arrogant. I can't stop my body from shivering. I don't know why he has this power over me. I know it's not because I want him again because I don't. I really don't. If he was the last man on earth, I wouldn't want him again. Okay, well, maybe that is a lie. If he was the last man on earth, I would definitely want him. And maybe even if he wasn't the last man on earth. If I just didn't have to know it was him, that would be fine. If he just kept his mouth shut and kept his belligerent, narcissistic comments to himself. I point at him and narrow my eyes. "I'm not going to sleep with you again. You wish, Colton Hart."

"I wouldn't say I wish. It wasn't totally unpleasant, of course. I wouldn't say no." He grins. "I mean, I'd do you again for sure."

"You'd do me again? Really? You are so crass."

"What would you rather me say? I'd fuck you again?"

I gasp and put my hands on my hips.

"That's not any better."

"Oh, okay," he says, lowering his voice until there's a silky hue to his tone. "Would you rather me say I'd like to make love to you, beautiful lady?"

I roll my eyes, and I can't stop a giggle at his southern tone. "You're stupid. You know that?"

"Well, I don't really think I agree with that. How many stupid people are billionaires?"

I just stare at him for a couple of seconds. One, because I'm shocked at how egotistical and arrogant he is and, two, because I hadn't realized he is a billionaire. I knew he was rich and a millionaire several times over, but a billionaire? Wow. I can't imagine having that amount of money.

My phone starts ringing, and I sigh as I glance at it. It's my parents.

"You should answer that," he says, nodding toward the screen.

"I don't think you can tell me what to do."

"Aw, are you going to be a petulant little girl? Are you not going to answer it just because I said you should?" He raises an eyebrow, and I answer the phone and then turn my back on him.

"Hello?" I say, sounding annoyed.

"Darling, we heard the good news," my mother says happily. I frown. What is she talking about? She doesn't know I slept with Colton, and I don't think she'd be calling to say that is good news. Especially if she knew how it went down.

"What, Mom? What good news?"

"We heard you got a job with Colton again. That he's giving you a second chance."

"What? Who told you that?"

"Your brother called us. Sam said that—"

"Mom, I think there's been a bit of a—"

"We're just so happy for you. We've been so stressed out since you lost your job. We know it's hard living in New York. Daddy even inquired last week about trying to get some extra money out of his 401(k) so we could send it to you. You know we don't have that much to live on right now. The economy is so bad. All our investments have gone down, and we're just not getting that much from Social Security. I know your brother has offered to help us, but..."

"Mom, it's..." I pause, feeling sick to my stomach. "You

don't have to go into your 401(k) to help me. I can find a job," I stammer.

"Well, you have a job now, silly. You're working for Colton Hart. We love him. When you see him, tell him we said thank you and we can't wait to see him this Christmas."

I hold in a deep sigh. I can hear Colton chuckling behind me. I'd forgotten that I had my volume on really high, so he could probably hear most of the conversation. I turn around and look at him, and he's dancing to the sound of music in his head. I glare at him. He winks. I stick my tongue out at him. He then wiggles his tongue at me, and all I can think about is his tongue in places that are currently wet.

"Mom, I don't know what to say," I say as he pulls off his shirt and throws it at me. I catch it and throw it back at him. He starts laughing, and I just shake my head.

"Where are you, darling? Is that a voice I hear in the background?" Why are my mom's ears so good?

"It's me, Mrs. Wynter!" Colton says loudly, and I glare at him as he steps toward me. I try not to look at his chest. He's way too sexy.

"Who's that, darling?"

"It's just Colton. I was with him because he needed to give me some work information," I say because that is much more preferable than telling her the truth.

"Oh, we don't want to disturb you while you're working. Give us a call when you're free. And be a good girl, Ella. Don't mess it up this time." My mom's voice is sweet.

"Mom, I didn't mess up the first time," I protest, but she doesn't want to hear it.

"Bye! Love you!" She hangs up, and I stare at Colton.

"You are a pig. And put your shirt on, please."

"Put my shirt on. What?" He flexes his biceps and then twitches his pecs, and I can feel my stomach twisting and turning. Why is he so handsome and so muscular? Why do I want to touch him?

"Yes, why did you take it off in the first place?"

"I mean, I can take off other items if you want, or you can take them off for me." He reaches down to his belt, and my fingers tremble.

"I'm not taking anything off for you, Colton Hart."

"Why do you like saying my name so much?"

"I don't. I don't like saying anything in regard to you at all. I don't even want to be here. This is a big mistake."

"Like I said, that's not what you were saying last night."

"Who says that anymore? We're not in high school or elementary school or..."

"Or what? I want you to answer one question. And then, if I believe you, we can let this whole thing go."

"Fine. What's the question?"

"You have to be honest, though."

"I'm always honest."

"Mm, sure." He cocks his head to the side and rolls his eyes.

"I'm always honest."

"Okay, then," he says. "Did I or did I not make you come more than you'd ever come before in your life last night?" He stares at me with his self-satisfied smile, and I want to scream. The truth of the matter is he's the best lover I've ever had, and there's no way I want him to know that. We stare at each other, and I can feel my heart racing. I watch as he unbuckles his belt, and I swallow hard. I have no idea how to answer his question.

6

"Ella." He grins, and I know that he is loving this. "You haven't answered my question." He starts dancing around, and I just stare at him. He's got more rhythm than I would have imagined him having.

"Do you want me to tell you that I think you're really immature?" I ask, and he bursts out laughing.

"I can call your parents right now if you want me to and tell them the truth."

"And just what would you say to my parents?"

"I don't know exactly. Maybe that you went to Sam's Christmas party and seduced me."

"I did not."

"Okay, I will say that you were dancing all sexy, we made out on the dance floor and I played with your tits, even though you supposedly didn't know who I was."

"I didn't." I blush at his words.

"Then I will tell them how you basically begged me to fuck you."

"I did not beg you for anything."

"Okay," he says, smiling. "Technically, you didn't *beg* beg, but we both know how badly you wanted it."

"Whatever. You wanted me."

"I did," he says, winking and coming closer to me. He grabs my hand, and I pull it away from him.

"What are you doing?"

"I would like a massage," he says, cocking his head to the side and looking me up and down. "If you're not going to vacuum and do the dishes, then at least give me a massage."

"What exactly is going on here?" I ask, gazing at him, glad he's forgotten about his question. "Are you really expecting me to be your assistant?"

"Your parents believe this is real, and that means I have to pay you. And if I have to pay you, you have to do a job. Don't worry, the pay is good."

"What are you going to pay me?" I ask, staring at him.

"I don't know. What about twenty-five thousand dollars a month?"

"Twenty-five thousand a month?" I squeal in surprise. My heart is giddy, and I almost want to laugh. "Are you kidding?"

"No, I wasn't kidding. Why? Are you hoping for more?"

"I mean..." I pause and stare at him. Twenty-five thousand dollars is more money than I've ever made in a month in my life. That will set me up for months. I can really and truly figure out what I want to do next. "I mean, whatever you think I'm worth," I say, gazing at him and shrugging. "You are a billionaire, after all."

He laughs lightly. "Okay, thirty grand a month, but no more. That should keep you going until you find a real job and—"

"So you admit I do need to find a real job?"

"I mean, unless you find a sugar daddy."

"Yeah, maybe I'll find a sugar daddy," I say, rolling my eyes.

"Well, you've tried before, haven't you?" he points out, and I just stare at him, shaking my head. I have no idea what he's talking about. "So, am I going to get that massage?" He starts pulling down his pants, and I gasp as he takes his boxers off as well. He's standing there naked in front of me. My mouth goes dry. I can't help but look at his cock. He's hard, and it's standing at attention, and I very much want to touch it, even though I don't really want him to know that I want to touch it. He takes another step closer to me. "So what's it to be, then?"

"What does that mean?" I ask, gazing at him. He looks like he wants to laugh. "I'm not giving you a blow job, if that's what you're asking."

"No, do we call your mom, or do I get my massage?"

"If I massage you, that's it. Doesn't mean I'm going down on you."

"That's not what I'm asking. Though, if you're offering," he looks down at his cock and then looks at my lips, "I wouldn't say no."

"I will give you a massage, but only because I want to make thirty grand. And after Christmas, once we've come back from my parents' house, this whole thing is done."

"Of course," he says, smiling. "If that's what you want. I mean, that was your plan after all, right?"

I just stare at him for a few seconds. I can't tell if he's being serious or not. Does he really think that I did this on purpose? Is his ego that big? A part of me wants to tell him off and leave, but I know I would be disappointing my parents. And thirty grand is a lot of money, and I need a lot of money. "Where do you want the massage?" I ask, changing the subject.

"Let's just go to the bedroom," he says. "Then, if you want to do anything else, it will be easier."

"What do you mean if I want to do anything else? Do you think this is some seedy massage parlor and I'm going to be one of those masseuses that's going to rub you and tug..." I pause. I don't even know what happens in those places.

"You sure about that?" he asks, and I roll my eyes as he walks toward his bedroom. I stare at his ass, and my eyes widen as I realize he has a tan line. His ass cheeks are super white, even though the rest of his body is a dark, golden tan. I giggle slightly as I notice.

"What's so funny?" he asks, glancing back at me.

"You don't want to know," I say, looking him up and down.

"Enjoying the view?"

I am enjoying the view, but I'm not going to tell him that. "I don't think so," I say as we walk into his bedroom. "Now get on the bed, close your eyes, and be quiet."

He smirks as he gets onto the bed, and I just stare at him for a couple of seconds. I am not sure exactly how I am going to massage him. This is slightly awkward. "Do you not want to put a towel down first or something?" I ask as he looks over at me. I thank God he's lying on his stomach and his back is toward me. Because if he was lying on his back and all I could see was his cock, I knew I would be in trouble. Even if I don't want to touch him and play with him, I have a feeling my fingers do, and I have a feeling other parts of my body do as well, if the tingling between my legs means anything.

"Why would I want to put a towel down?"

"I don't know. Because I was going to use baby oil to massage you."

"Really? You want me all slippery, huh?"

"No, I don't want you in any way. In fact, I'd rather go home and watch TV, but..." I shrug. "Do you have any baby oil?"

"You can look in the bathroom," he says. "Bring a towel out as well and feel free to take your clothes off if you want."

"You wish." I head into his bathroom and look around. Of course, it's huge and marble and the place of many women's fantasies with its large claw-foot tub that one could soak in for hours and hours. There is a walk-in shower that also makes my knees weak when I see the sit-in bench. "Wow," I mumble under my breath. Must be nice to be so rich. I open some drawers and finally happen upon some Johnson's baby oil. I don't want to know why he has it. Actually, I can most probably figure out why he has it, but I don't want to think about that. I head back into the bedroom, and he looks at me.

"Found it?"

"Yes, I did." I squeeze some into my hands and rub his shoulders, massaging him as hard as I can. He groans as my fingers run up and down his back.

"That feels so good," he says with his eyes closed.

"I'm sure it does." I realize I can't massage his lower back properly from my stance at the side of the bed, so I slip off my shoes and get onto the bed, kneeling beneath his ass. I move my fingers up and down, rubbing and kneading, and I can tell he is enjoying it.

"So you didn't answer my question." He grunts. "Have you ever come that much in your life before?"

I glare at his back, annoyed by the tone in his voice that tells me he already knows the answer.

"And you have to be honest."

"I don't really remember," I lie. "So I can't answer."

"Liar." He chuckles. "I had you gushing like Niagara Falls."

I ignore him as my fingers get closer to his ass cheeks, and a sudden naughty idea pops into my mind. I grin to myself as my fingers rub him. I am going to teach Colton Hart a lesson. I start to massage his butt cheeks, and I can tell that he's not expecting that. He looks back over at me with a raised eyebrow. "You don't have to massage my butt if you don't want to."

"Oh no. I feel like you deserve a proper massage. You deserve all of this," I say as I run my fingers back and forth and knead my thumbs into his muscles. He shrugs and presses his face back into the mattress. I continue to massage him up and down for a couple of minutes, and then I let my finger slip all the way down and hover it close to his asshole. I press it in slightly, and he jumps up off the bed in shock.

"What the hell?" he shouts, looking at me, and I giggle slightly.

"Oops, sorry. My finger slipped."

"Were you about to put your finger in my butthole?" He stares at me and gets back onto the bed, only this time, he's on his back and staring up at me. I lick my lips nervously and try not to look at his cock as he adjusts himself. This is so unprofessional.

"Don't look. Don't look," I mumble to myself.

"What?" he asks, and I see his wrist moving up and down. Is he jacking off?

"No, not at all. Of course I wasn't trying to do that," I say as my eyes look at his cock getting harder. "I would not slip a finger in your ass."

"Uh-huh." He groans, and his fingers pause and drop to the side. He grunts and closes his eyes. "You can continue to massage the rest of me now."

"Sure," I say as I shift up slightly. His cock is right there in front of me, and I'm not sure how to massage him without some part of my body touching it. I run my fingers up and down his chest, admiring his abs. I move my fingers close to his cock and balls but don't touch them. I can feel his body getting harder. More rigid. And I know he wants me to touch him. I enjoy the fact that I'm getting so close but not actually relieving him of any of his horniness.

Five minutes pass, and his eyes pop open. "You know, you can touch me if you want to." He nods toward his cock. "I don't mind."

"I don't think so." I shake my head and sit back as if I'm shocked by his comment.

"If you want to give me a blow job or even have a little bounce, go ahead," he says a few minutes later. There's a devilish smirk on his face and I know he's trying to wind me up.

"Have a little bounce?" I stare at him with my best stern and disapproving headmaster look. "Really?"

"Hey." He grins. "You seem to like to do the work. I bet your pussy is all wet for me, like—"

"Enough," I cut him off. "We are not to talk about that ever again. You hear me?"

"Fine," he says. "I mean, you've got me all horny for my date tonight. I was hoping that you'd relieve me from some of this lust."

"Your date tonight?" I stare at him in surprise. I still cannot believe it.

"Yeah. Why? Are you jealous?"

"No. Why would I be jealous? I literally could not care less if you're going on a date. I mean, I hope you enjoy yourself because I'm sure she won't."

"Oh, I'm pretty sure she's going to enjoy herself a lot," he says, grinning at me. "I think most women enjoy their time with me."

"Okay. If you say so."

"I'm sure she's going to be screaming out my name when I make her come."

"You're full of yourself, and I'm pretty sure she's not going to be doing any of that."

"Oh yeah? You mean like you weren't screaming my name last night when you were coming hard and fast?"

"I'm just saying I can fake it as well as every other woman on the planet."

He sits up, then, and glares at me. "You're such a liar."

"No, I'm not lying. Maybe your ego can't take the fact that I faked it, but I did."

"I could rip off your panties right now and taste your wetness, Ella," he says. "Do you want me to do that?"

"No," I growl, even though my brain is screaming, *yes, yes, yes*. He pushes me back down on the mattress, and we just glare at each other. He leans over and moves my skirt up, and I don't stop him. His cock is resting next to my thigh, and I shift slightly. Colton's hand slips down the front of my skirt, and he rubs his fingers between my legs. I moan slightly, and he grins. I don't stop him when he pulls my skirt all the way down and onto the ground. I'm lying there in my panties, and I groan as he hovers over me, brushing his cock against the material. He kisses the side of my face as he grinds into me. His cock thrusts against my panties, and my entire body is shaking. He reaches up and pulls my panties down, reaching his fingers across my wetness.

"Not interested at all, eh?" he says as he gently rubs my clit.

I'm thankful when my phone starts ringing, and I answer it quickly. "Hello?" I say, glaring at Colton as he stares at me, his fingers rubbing me tenderly.

"Hey, I just wanted to make sure everything was okay." It's Danny, and I try not to groan.

"Oh, I'm good. Thank you. Just working." I press down on my lips as Colton spreads my legs and leans down.

"Oh, you are such a hard worker. I really appreciate you coming over and looking after Frannie. It's always a pleasure when you're here."

"Oh, I love her. She's so sweet. I really hope to have a little girl like her one day." I gasp as I feel Colton's face between my legs; his tongue is on my clit, and my body is shaking.

"You never know. Maybe your dreams will come true," Danny says and pauses. Colton's tongue thrusts into me, and I gasp. "Is everything okay, Ella?" Danny sounds worried, and I can barely think. Colton's tongue is now flicking against my clit, and I want to scream.

"Hey, Danny, I, I...ooh...I...fu..." I grab Colton's head and pull it away. I'm about to orgasm, and I do not want Danny to hear me. Colton grabs his cock and rubs it against my entrance, and I moan as I feel the head of him about to enter me. I know I should push him away, but I want to feel him inside of me.

"So, Ella, I was wondering if..." Danny starts, but I can't concentrate.

"I haven't finished work yet. Can I speak to you later?"

"Sure," he says, sounding peeved. "Sorry to disturb you." I can tell he's slightly aggravated, though I'm not sure why. I just don't have time to think about it right now.

"Well, speak to you soon," I say and hang up. Colton grabs my hands and kisses me on the lips.

"I knew you were horny as soon as you walked in." He chuckles, his cock about to thrust inside of me. I sigh and push him to the side.

"You have to stop being so obnoxious when I'm on the phone." I jump off the bed and reach for my panties and skirt.

"Okay, and who were you just talking to?" He stares at me, grabs my hand, and pulls me back onto the bed.

"I was just speaking to Danny. He's Frannie's father, the little girl I was babysitting when you so rudely called me this afternoon." I gasp as he spreads my legs again and hovers over me.

"I'd watch what you say to him," Colton says as his cock rubs my clit.

"Excuse me?" I stare at him, trying to still my rapidly racing heart. I can feel that I'm about to orgasm.

"I'm just saying. You keep making comments like that and he's going to think you want to be that little girl's new mama."

"Whatever," I say, rolling my eyes, and I gasp as he grabs my fingers and puts them on his cock. I run my fingers up and down as he slips a finger inside of me. Within minutes, we're both coming, and I can barely breathe. He then pulls me into his arms and presses his lips against mine. I can feel his cock pressed up against my stomach, and I kiss him back. I know I shouldn't be doing this, but I can't stop myself. His body is hard and oily, and I melt against him. He slips his tongue into my mouth, and I suck on it. As he runs his hands down my back, I feel them on my ass. He squeezes my ass cheeks as he pushes me in closer to him. He reaches around and tries to press a finger into my asshole. His eyes are glittering as he stares at me, and I gasp.

"You wanna feel my cock in your ass?" he asks with a chuckle, and something snaps inside of me because, yes, I'm curious as to what it would feel like. But I'm not going to give him the satisfaction.

I push him away and just shake my head. "Have fun on your date," I say, getting off the bed again. "Maybe she'll let you fuck her ass. As for me, I'm leaving now."

7

I feel proud of myself as I make my way back to my apartment. I still can't quite believe that I left Colton standing there, and I can still hear his chuckles as I exit, but I know I don't want him to get the better of me. I still can't believe I let him take my panties off again that quickly, but he really is hard to resist.

I think about Danny and his phone call and the way he'd been acting in the apartment before I'd left him and Frannie. I wonder if he is somehow getting the wrong impression, but I dismiss those thoughts from my mind. Danny is just a client, and I'm someone he can count on to help with Frannie. I'm glad he has me. And I know I need to stop overthinking everything, like wondering who Colton is going on a date with this evening.

Poor girl. She has no clue that he was just trying to fuck me. He's so trashy. I can't believe he had me massage him and then went down on me while I was on the phone. He's the epitome of a player. Isabel would call him a fuckboy.

I open the door to my apartment, walk inside, and head over to the couch to turn the TV on. I'm looking forward to watching something mindless, maybe a dating show or a

British murder mystery. For some reason, I've really gotten into watching British murder mysteries in the last couple of months. I am almost through all the seasons of *Midsomer Murders* and *Rosemary and Thyme*. I turn on the TV and flick to BritBox so I can lose myself in the English countryside.

My phone starts ringing, and I smile when I see that it's Isabel. I pick up the phone. "Hey, chica, how's it going?"

"Hey there, Ella. I was just wondering how you're feeling about *everything*." There's a mischievous tone to her voice, and I know she wants to say something else but is holding herself back. I also know that by "everything," she wants to know how I feel about banging Colton. She's been listening to me complain about him for years, so I know she's as shocked as I am by what's happened.

"I still feel like I made a huge mistake," I say, groaning, the sound resembling something that would come out of an old donkey's stomach. "You won't believe what happened today."

"Oh, no. You didn't hook up with him again, did you?"

"No, of course not. I wouldn't do such a thing," I say, though I'm not sure if that's exactly true. I was half tempted this afternoon. And did his going down on me count as hooking up? Technically, I think it does, but I don't want to be technical.

"So tell me, what have you been up to?" she asks. "What happened?"

"You know I was babysitting Frannie this afternoon."

"Yeah, and how did that go?" I can tell that she's not really interested, but she's still asking. Isabel is the face of politeness in all ways, except for when we go drinking.

"Fine. She's such a sweet girl. Anyway, Danny came home early, and I ended up having to go over to Colton's because he called me and demanded I come over right then,"

I say by way of explanation. I need her to know that I didn't just show up because I wanted to.

"Why exactly did you go to Colton's?"

"Because he called me and made it seem like there was some sort of emergency," I say. "He was like, 'You need to get over here right now,' and I thought perhaps Sam found out something." I try not to groan at the mention of my brother. I don't know what Sam will do if he finds out that I hooked up with Colton. I wonder if that fear will ever dissipate.

"Oh no, he didn't find out, did he?" Isabel seems far too excited to be talking about Sam, and I wonder if she's interested in him in a romantic sense.

"No, Colton was just being a jackass and was like, 'Why didn't you tidy up my place?' And I was like, 'Excuse me?' and he was like, 'Well, you're my assistant,' and I was like, 'But I don't want to be,' and then my mom called."

"Oh, what did your mom say?"

"Stupid Sam told her that I got my job back with Colton, so she was all excited. I was about to tell her that it actually wasn't going to work out, and then she told me that she and my dad were going to break into their 401(k) to help me financially. I can't do that to them. I know how tough things have been, and I know the economy sucks." I let out a long, deep sigh.

"Oh, no," she says. "So you pretended that you were working for him?"

"Yep, and Colton is going to pay me."

"Whoa, like a real salary?" She sounds as shocked as I felt. "How much? A grand a week?"

"Girl, he said he's going to pay me thirty grand."

"A year?"

"A month."

"Oh my gosh, you're not like a paid escort or something, are you?" she shrieks, and I giggle slightly.

"No, what are you talking about?"

"I'm just saying, is he paying you to be his assistant, or is he paying you for sex?"

"Isabel, I cannot believe you would even ask that. I slept with him already, and I didn't get paid, and if I did sleep with him again, it wouldn't be because of the money."

"So you admit there's a possibility that you would sleep with him again?"

"I mean, I don't know. Times are rough 'round here, and if I have a drink, or I get lonely or horny, or... It could happen, but it won't be because of money."

"Okay," she says, "no need to be so defensive."

"You would be defensive, as well, if I asked you if you were considering a life as a prostitute."

"Okay, fine. That's not exactly what I was saying, but—"

"But anyways, he started doing a striptease for me while I was on the phone with my mom."

"Oh my gosh, no way."

"I know, and then he asked me to give him a massage."

"And you told him no?"

"Oh, I gave him a massage, all right, and then my finger accidentally slipped." I giggle.

"What? What do you mean it accidentally slipped? Slipped where?"

"Nearly slipped into his butthole." I burst out laughing. "He jumped so high. I thought it was hilarious."

"Wow. I cannot believe you did that."

"Why not?" I say. "He thinks he's in control and I'm some little fool that's going to act all shy and embarrassed. I'm not shy because I slept with him. I'm just pissed off because it was with him."

"I know, girl. You don't like him."

"I have reason to not like him."

"Trust me, I know, Ella. I agree with you. He treated you so poorly in the past. But you do have to admit he's a hottie."

"Well, obviously, I think he's a hottie, or I wouldn't have

slept with him." I sigh. "But it's not going to happen again. I'm just going to be his assistant and do whatever I've got to do, aside from sleep with him, of course. Then we'll go to Christmas in Florida, which, by the way, I've been looking on Instagram, and everyone's lives are so glamorous. Really makes me feel like I am such a loser."

"You're not a loser, though."

"Compared to everyone else I went to high school with, I'm the biggest loser going."

"Oh, Ella, don't feel that way."

"I know I shouldn't, but no man, no money, no nothing. I cannot go back home and meet up with those girls and show them who I am."

"Then what are you going to do?"

"I need to find someone to take with me or win the lottery."

"Good luck with that," she says, laughing.

"Yeah, I know. It's very unlikely to happen, but maybe there's a unicorn out there somewhere waiting to make my dreams come true."

"A unicorn?" she asks.

"I don't know. I'm tired." I laugh. "I don't even know what I'm saying. I'm just going to watch some TV now and go to bed early." I yawn loudly.

"Okay, sweet dreams. Want to hang out tomorrow?"

"Sounds good." I hang up and lean back into the couch. I decide to watch some episodes of *Rules of Engagement*, one of my favorite TV sitcoms, instead of the murder mystery. "I should go to bed." I yawn without moving from the couch. I don't have a TV near my bed, so I decide to stay where I am. My mind flashes to Colton again and how confusing everything is. Then I wonder how his date is going and if he's going to sleep with her.

I must drift to sleep because my ringing phone wakes me up at one a.m. I groan when I see that it is Colton. "Why are you calling me? I thought you had a date," I mumble as I stare at the phone. I am not going to answer it. However, as it continues ringing, I can feel a twinge of something in my heart, but I don't know what it is. I know it's not jealousy. I don't care how many women he dates. He can date all of the women in Manhattan, Queens, Staten Island, and Brooklyn, and I won't care. I stare at the phone and let it ring and go to voice mail. "I'm not answering," I say, even though the phone is no longer ringing. I don't want to hear about his date.

I am about to turn the phone off when it starts ringing again. I feel nervous for a few moments as I contemplate other reasons why he may be calling. "What if he's calling about Sam? Shit, what if something happened to Sam?" I talk out loud, jump up and pace back and forth before grabbing the phone reluctantly. "Hello," I mutter into the phone, annoyed that he's gotten me to answer him again.

"What are you doing?" he asks, sounding slightly irritated. "You took forever to answer."

"What do you mean, what am I doing?" I look at my watch. "It's one o'clock in the morning. Is Sam okay?" I snap.

"Yeah. Why would you ask me that?"

"Then why are you calling me at one a.m.?" I'm irritated now.

"Because I need you to do something for me."

"Are you joking?"

"Why would I be joking? Are you or are you not my assistant, making thirty grand a month?"

"Really, Colton?" I can hear my voice rising like I'm practicing the scales.

"What?" he says. "I can pay you less if you want, but if I'm paying you thirty grand, you will be available to me when I need you."

I bite down on my lower lip. "What is it you want?" I can

barely control my anger, and I very much want to tell him to go and take a long walk off a short cliff. A very short cliff.

"I need you to run an errand."

"What? Right now?" I'm pissed. If he asks me to bring him a burger and fries, I will scream.

"Yes, right now." He's chuckling now like it's funny. It's then that I notice I can hear music in the background and some girls laughing.

"Where are you?" I ask him, frowning.

"I'm out at a club."

"You are out at a club? Then why the hell are you calling me, the person who's home and in bed sleeping, to run an errand? Are you out of your mind?"

"Nah, not out of my mind. I need you to go and buy me a box of rubbers." He chuckles again, and I freeze.

"What?" My jaw drops. "Are you freaking kidding me?"

"I used up my last condoms with you last night, and well, I want to take my date home and—"

"You want me to go and buy you a box of condoms for your date?"

"Hey, you speak English, and you finally understand. Great. Go and get them and be at my place within forty-five minutes." He hangs up, and I just stare at the phone. I power it off and head toward my bedroom. I cannot believe the nerve of this man. He really thinks I'm going to buy him condoms? I'm so angry that I cannot think straight. I am so pissed off that I start fluffing my pillows really hard into the mattress, imagining they are his face. I'm also kind of jealous, not because I like him, but because he just slept with me and now he wants to sleep with someone else. Was it really that unmemorable to him? Am I really not that special? I mean, I know I'm not special, but I feel like there should be some time period after me.

I'm about to get into bed when an idea crosses my mind. I smile to myself, grab a sweater and head toward the door with my handbag. I know I'm being immature, but I don't care. I head down to the corner store and look around for what I want, find a box, pick it up, and pay for it. Then I make my way to Colton's apartment. I'm curious to see what his date looks like. If she's pretty. She's most probably gorgeous, a supermodel, or an actress, or something. That's when I do feel a slight amount of jealousy, but not because I care. I really don't care. I just wish that I had more of a life than to be headed out doing his errands at this time of night.

I ring the doorbell and bang on the door loudly as I get to his place. He answers it and stares at me in my disheveled state. "You got the stuff?"

"Yes," I say, glaring at him.

"Come on in, then."

"What do you mean, 'Come on in'? I'm just going to give it to you, and then—"

"Inside," he says.

I step inside the apartment and frown. "You're such a jackass. You know that, right?"

"I think you may have told me that once or twice before."

"Whatever. Where's the date?" I say, looking around. The apartment is oddly quiet.

"I changed my mind," he says, looking at me.

"What, and you didn't think to tell me?"

"Well, I didn't know if you actually would do the errand for me, and the last thing I want is to get some rando pregnant or catch an STD."

I stare at him, my mouth agape. "You are disgusting."

"Hey, but I am feeling horny still, so if you want to join me in the bedroom"—he winks—"then hey, we could make sure that we're protected."

"Actually, I don't think that's a good idea," I say, shaking my head.

He stares at me for a couple of seconds. "What do you mean?"

"I mean, if you take me to the bedroom and try and have your wicked way with me, you're essentially telling me that you want me to get pregnant and have your baby."

"What the hell are you talking about?" I giggle as I hold out the plastic bag and hand it to him. He pulls out the box and stares at it. "Balloons? You got me balloons?" His eyes narrow. "Is this meant to be a joke?"

"Yep," I say, smiling at him. "I figured, hey, what's the difference for a man like you?"

"You got me balloons instead of condoms?" He grins suddenly, and I'm not sure why he thinks this is funny. "You were really jealous," he says, laughing. "I knew it."

"What do you mean?" I roll my eyes. "No, I wasn't jealous."

"I think you were. That's why you didn't want me to get laid tonight."

"Honestly, I couldn't care less," I say, shaking my head. "You can call her right now if you want."

"And do what? I don't even have any condoms. These balloons are obviously not going to work."

"Oh, well, I guess you'll have to figure it out," I say, looking at my watch. "I think I'm going to go home now. Have a good evening, Blue Balls Colton."

He stares at me for a couple of seconds and shakes his head. "You want to stay over?" he asks softly.

I stare at him for a couple of seconds. "No."

He puts his hand against the wall and runs a finger down the side of my face. I shiver slightly as he comes closer to me. "You want to stay over?"

"You don't have any condoms, so..." I shrug.

"There are other things we can do," he says, his right hand moving down to my breast and squeezing. I don't stop him. I like the feel of his hand against me. I don't know what he's doing, but it feels like magic.

"I shouldn't stay. You know that."

"No, I don't know anything," he says. He grabs my hand and pulls me toward the bedroom. "I mean, technically, we're still in the same time period of when we already fucked, so..." He shrugs, looking at me.

I stare at him for a few seconds and take a deep breath. "I'm not interested, Colton. I am going home."

"Oh, okay," he says, "because I really wanted to..." He pauses and licks his lips.

"You really wanted to what?" I ask him, curiosity winning out.

"I really wanted you to sit on my face and come for me," he says, grinning. I just stare at him, and he bursts out laughing.

8

"Hey, I have an idea," Isabel says as we chow down on our sandwiches.

"What's the idea?" I ask her suspiciously. Whenever Isabel has an idea, I start to worry. Not because she doesn't have good intentions but because her ideas always seem to work out in a way that doesn't quite benefit me.

"So you said you wanted to meet a guy to take back with you to Florida."

"I mean, I was kind of joking. I am going back home in a couple of weeks. Let's be real. I'm not going to find someone who's going to come with me to Florida already. That would be weird."

"You never know."

"What do you mean I never know?"

"Girl, haven't you seen that show on TV about women that meet their soul mate and know it after the first date?"

"No, I've never heard of such a show," I say. "Why?"

"Well, there's a speed-dating event tomorrow, and I thought we should go."

"What? Speed dating." I look at her before taking a

bite of my BLT. I chew on the salty bacon and swallow before I answer her. "I don't know how I feel about speed dating."

"I bet you can meet a really eager guy," she says, gazing at me as she eats a french fry.

"And what does an eager guy equal?"

"I don't know. What does an eager guy equal? An eager guy equals someone who's going to go with you back to Florida and show all your snooty high school friends that you are living your best life."

"I guess."

"It'll be fun. Just dress to the nines and look sexy as hell. I guarantee you are going to meet a really great guy."

"I don't know that you can actually guarantee that, but I suppose it's worth a try."

"Yes, it is. So, how's Colton, by the way?"

"Let's just call him the boss."

"The boss," she says, giggling. "So that's his new name?"

"Yeah, we can just call him TB."

"TB like tuberculosis?"

"Or we can just call him B," I say.

"No, because when you say B, it makes me think a bitch, and he's not a bitch."

"Well, he is kind of a bitch," I say, and she laughs.

"What about if we call him BB?"

"Like BB gun?" I ask her.

"No, big boss."

"Why? Because he has a big cock?" I ask, and then my face goes red and she giggles.

"You never told me that part. Please give me all the information."

"Isabel, I'm not talking about Colton Hart's cock. Be it small, medium, or large."

"I think you confirmed just now that it was large," she says. "Come on, I'm your best friend."

"I mean, fine, it was larger than it should be because he doesn't deserve to have one."

"That amazing?"

I groan. "Oh my gosh. I sound like a fool."

"No, you don't. You sound like someone that got loved real good."

"Trust me, there was nothing loving about what we did."

"It was giving, though, huh?" She winks at me, and I shake my head.

"I'm not talking about this anymore. Nope, nope, nope." I look down at my phone and see that Danny has texted me. "Oh, hold on a second, let me see what Danny wants. He may want me to babysit for Frannie again."

"He really counts on you a lot."

"I know, but he doesn't have anyone else that he trusts as much as me. And you know, poor Frannie."

"I know Frannie's mom ran out." Isabel holds her hands up. "Look, I'm not trying to be insensitive to the fact that the girl lost her mom, but you are not the surrogate mom, and he doesn't even pay you that well, does he?"

"I mean, he pays okay." I sigh. "Actually, he doesn't want me to babysit," I say, looking at the text message. "He wants to know what I'm doing tomorrow evening."

"Oh, well, you're busy, right?" Isabel stares at me, and I just nod slowly.

"Fine. I will come to the speed-dating event, but I don't expect anything to come of it."

"Okay. And if it doesn't, then maybe you can just meet up with Colton."

"I thought we were calling him BB."

"I thought you didn't want to call him BB."

"Actually, let's call him BB."

"Oh yeah. And why is that? What made you change your mind?" she asks.

"I don't want to call him BB for big boss. I want to call him BB for blue balls."

"Oh my gosh. What?"

"It's an inside joke. One that I don't want to talk about right now." I think back to Colton and the way I left him the evening before. "Let's just say he's not going to be asking me to buy him condoms anytime soon."

"He what?" she asks, and I just giggle.

"Now show me more information about this event so I know what I'm getting myself into."

❅

"You look so hot," Isabel says as I meet her outside of the club where the speed-dating event is going to be held. "Mamacita, you are smoking."

"Thank you. You're not looking so bad yourself," I say as I stare at her in her slinky red dress. "We are definitely both fire."

"Oh yeah, we are," she says. "All the other women are going to be so jealous because we are going to get all the hotties if there are any hotties," I say. "Shall we go inside?"

"Let's do it. Oh my gosh. I'm so excited. Aren't you?"

"No, I think I need a drink or two, and this time, at least, I know I'm not wearing a mask when no one else is."

"What does that have to do with anything?" she asks curiously.

"So I don't go home with anyone crazy." I stare at her like she's stupid. "How can you forget?"

"But you knew who he was before you went home with him, right?"

I glare at her. "Yes, I knew, but that was after I had already made out with him, bumping and grinding on the dance floor."

"Well, hey, maybe it was a good thing you had on a mask. At least you got some."

"I got some with a man who fired me after one hour. Who is now making me work for him and do crazy chores in the middle of the night just because he has the power to do so."

"Yeah, but he's also paying you thirty grand."

"Speaking of which," I say, "I haven't received any money yet. Hold on, let me text him." I grab his number in my phone and send him a quick text. "Hey, just wondering when I'm going to get paid." I press send and then look over at Isabel. "Okay, come on, let's go." The club is dark as we make our way inside, and I can barely see what is going on. "Oh my gosh. Is it going to be a bunch of uggos?" I ask, looking at Isabel.

"Why'd you ask that?" she asks, grabbing my hand.

"Because we can't see anything."

"Oh, it's just mood lighting, and hey, it helps us, too. We're going to look like a billion dollars in this light."

"So what are you saying? We normally look like ten cents?"

"No." She grins. "We don't normally look like ten cents, but let's be real. We don't look like a billion dollars. Maybe more like a million."

"Nice save," I say, laughing as we head toward the bar.

"Shall we get a drink first?" she asks. "Then we'll look for the organizer."

"Sounds good." We wait for the bartender to serve us, and then we get two lemon drop martinis. I take a couple of sips and feel myself relaxing. There's just something about alcohol and sugar that takes me to my happy place.

"Oh, look, there are the tables." Isabel points to the corner, and we head over there. I can see a gaggle of women standing to one side, and across from them are about eight men. I try not to look them up and down too closely. I don't want them to think I'm too eager or checking them out. I feel a sense of worry as I stand there, and I'm not sure why. "This is going to be so exciting," Isabel says.

"Yeah, I guess." My phone beeps, and I look down at it. It's Colton. "Oh, he says that he will pay me tomorrow if I want to come over."

"Oh, girl, he just wants you to get into his bed. Do you even know what your chores are going to be?"

"What do you mean, my chores? Do you mean my work duties?"

"Oh yeah, sorry, I used the wrong term."

"Really, Isabel?"

"What? I mean, it did seem like you were going to act more like a housekeeper than an admin person." I just stare at her. I don't want to get into an argument, and I don't want to think about the last time I worked for Colton. That was so embarrassing, and I still don't really understand why I got fired.

"Hey, everyone." A lady with long, red hair steps toward the group. "Can everyone step forward for me? My name is Jimena. Nice to meet you all. I'm sure you're really excited about our speed-dating event tonight. Here's how it's going to work. Ladies, you're going to take a seat at one of the tables, and you're going to be able to speak to each guy for about four minutes. When we ring the bell, gentlemen, you're going to get up and switch tables. Ladies and gentlemen, you'll both make a note on the paper that we provide and state whether or not you would like to see that person again. At the end of the night, we will match up who would like to see whom again, and then you can go on a second date and possibly, maybe, find the love of your life." She laughs. "And if you do, I hope to be invited to the wedding."

"You'll definitely be invited to mine," a cute blonde purrs from next to us. She's definitely here to find herself a man to marry as soon as possible. All of us women laugh. I look over at the men and can see they feel nervous.

"Why is it that guys come to these things, yet they never seem like they want to get married?" I whisper to Isabel.

"Because they think they're going to get some easy sex," she says and rolls her eyes.

"I just don't get guys. Like, why come to an event hoping to have a one-night stand, but you know the women are looking for commitment?" I sigh. "Well, hey, at least Colton's not here."

"Well, you never know," she says, and I look at the guys quickly, my heart racing. She giggles. "He's not here. Don't worry, Ella."

"You nearly scared me. If he was here, I was going to leave. You know that, right?"

"I know, but," she says, winking at me, "most probably, you'd be leaving just so you could go back to his place."

"Isabel. Really?"

"What? Now that I know that he's packing, I understand why he's got you all flustered and confused."

"He does not have me flustered and confused." I glare at her.

"He is a jackass. We both know it, but you still slept with him, and you are now his assistant. Like, assistant of what?"

"Like I said, that's what I need to find out as well."

"Okay." She shrugs. "But maybe tonight you can meet a real man that will make you forget Colton and make you want to..." She pauses as Jimena claps her hands.

"Okay, ladies, everyone go and take a table," she says and points toward the tables. I walk toward one at the back, pull out the stool and sit down. Isabel sits at the table next to me. A bell rings, and a tall man comes and stands next to the table, then takes a seat.

"Hi," he says, his voice deep. "Nice to meet you."

"Nice to meet you, too," I say as he sits down. He's very attractive, though he looks slightly older.

"What's your name?" he asks.

"I'm Ella."

"Oh, cute. Hi, Ella."

"And your name?" I prod him.

"Oh, sorry, I forgot to say, it's George."

"Oh, cool. Like George Clooney? Very nice," I say, nodding. He isn't as handsome as George Clooney, but he is still not bad. I smile to myself. If all the men are this attractive, then maybe this isn't going to be such a bad evening after all.

"So I'm going to be really honest with you, Emma."

"It's Ella."

"Yeah, Emma. I'm going to be honest with you," he says, leaning forward to take a sip of his beer.

"Okay, cool, and that honesty entails?"

"I'm just getting out of a relationship. I was married for fifteen years."

"Fifteen years." I blink. So, how old is this man?

"Yeah, and we have three kids, and obviously, they're still going to come first in my life, but"—he pauses—"I'm always available for midnight screwing."

"You're what?" I say, blinking. Did I hear him right?

"I said I'm always available for midnight screwing."

"Screwing?" I repeat.

"Yeah, or what do you say these days? Fucking?"

I take a long gulp of my lemon drop. Okay, so maybe this isn't going to go as well as I hoped. "I'm not really looking for that," I say, shaking my head. "Sorry."

"Oh, well, what were you looking for? Maybe we can find a place to meet in the middle," he says, grinning as he chugs more of his beer.

"Honestly, I'm looking for a man to come with me to Florida in a couple of weeks to meet my parents and my high school friends, and hopefully, he'll propose to me in front of them with a huge diamond ring." I beam at him. "You think that's something you'd be interested in doing?" His eyes widen, and I burst out laughing.

"That's a joke, right?" he says. "You're a comedian or something."

"No, it's not a joke, and I'm not a comedian," I say, grinning. "But if you're not interested, I'm sure I will be able to find someone else who will be."

"Oh my gosh. You women are crazy these days."

"Is it making you think about going back to your ex-wife?" He pauses and takes another sip of his beer.

"Okay. I mean, it doesn't seem like we're going to hit it off, right?"

"No, we're definitely not going to hit it off."

"And if I'm honest, she's not exactly my ex-wife."

"Okay, your wife that you're separated from, right?"

"Well, maybe she doesn't really know that we're separated."

My jaw drops. "Then what the—"

"I'm just in town with my buddies for the week, and I thought I could meet a girl who wanted to have some fun. No strings attached. I've got three kids. I haven't had sex in two weeks." I just stare at him and shake my head.

"Oh my gosh. You are literally horrible."

"Well, it's a good thing that we didn't hit it off, then, right?" He winks. The bell rings, and I'm grateful when he stands up and moves to the next table. I am literally going to murder Isabel for bringing me here. If all the men are as bad as this, it is going to be a long night. The next guy sits at the table and smiles at me. He kind of reminds me of Will Smith, and I wonder if he's going to be nice or...

"Hi," he says, "my name's Russell."

"Nice to meet you. I'm Ella," I say, stressing the la part of my name. "With two *L*'s and not two *M*'s."

"Got it," he nods, "Ella, not Emma."

"Yep," I smile, hoping I'm not coming across as a condescending biatch. "So are you still married or...?"

He frowns slightly and shakes his head. "No, I wouldn't be here if I was married. Why? Are you?"

"No, but the first guy I spoke to was still married and looking to cheat on his wife with me, so..."

"Oh no, that's not me. Actually, I haven't dated anyone in a while." He grins. "What about you?"

"No, I haven't dated anyone in what could be referred to as a hot minute."

"Well, I guess I haven't dated anyone in what could be referred to as a cold minute," he says, and we both laugh. "So what do you do for a living, Ella?"

I pause. "I am an assistant right now to a billionaire, which sounds a lot fancier than it is. What about you?"

"I am actually an accountant," he says, "which also sounds fancier than it is." He looks at me, and his eyes crinkle. "So you're very pretty and you're funny. What are your flaws?"

"You think I'm pretty?" I say, flirting back at him. Maybe this guy isn't so bad after all. He is cute, and I also think he has a great sense of humor.

"I said it, right?" He beams at me. "This is really awkward, isn't it?"

"Yes, my friend made me come. What about you?" I ask.

"Actually, I made my friend come," he says, laughing. "We don't seem to have the best luck meeting ladies. So I thought, what about a speed-dating event? This way, we get to date several women at one time without being douchebags."

"Is that the way you see it?"

"Plus, I get to see if I like them and they like me." He holds his glass up. "You want to cheers to the evening?"

"Sure," I say, holding my martini glass up. We cheers, and I take a sip.

"What's that you're drinking?" he asks, nodding over at my glass.

"It's a lemon drop martini," I say. "Sweet and sour, a little bit like me."

"Ooh. Is that a warning?"

"No. Do you not like being sweet and sour?"

"I think I like to change it up every now and again, so I do think I could deal with that," he says. "I like you, Ella. You're fun."

"Thank you. I think you seem kind of cool right now, too, even though you're only the second guy I've met tonight."

"Well, I hope you check my name off," he says, "because I will certainly be checking yours off."

"Well, thank you, Russell."

"You're welcome." The bell rings, and he stands up and bows his head. "Hopefully, I'll get to see you again later."

"I hope so, too," I say, looking at him happily. Maybe, just maybe, he will be a good guy. I don't know what to think, but I am open to it. Colton's face pops into my head, and I frown. I do not want to think about Colton Hart at all. As far as I am concerned, the other night never happened.

9

The next couple of dates go as I expect them to go. Most of the guys are insufferable and full of themselves. I take a sip of my drink and lean back. I look over and see how it's going for everyone else. Isabel is giggling at something the guy in front of her is saying, and I wonder if she finds him funny or if she's just drunk.

"Well, I don't believe it," a voice says, and I look back in front of me. My eyes widen as I see Danny sitting there.

"Hey," I say in surprise.

"Hey, you," he says, sitting back, running his fingers through his hair. "I can't believe that you're at a speed-dating event."

"Yeah, it was Isabel's idea," I say. "I didn't know you were going to be here, either. Who's looking after Frannie?"

"Oh, she's at a friend's house for the evening," he says, leaning forward. He looks me up and down and then bites down on his lower lip. His eyes are wide with mirth. "This is a little bit awkward, isn't it?" he says. "I don't know if I should flirt. It's a bit inappropriate to flirt with my babysitter."

"I guess we can just chat," I say, shrugging. Danny is

cute, but he's not my type. And while I love Frannie, I'm not looking to be a stepmom anytime soon. Plus, he's right. A babysitter and a dad should not cross that line. I mean, it happens all the time, but I don't know that it's professional.

"So, Ella," he says, licking his lips, "have you ever partaken in sixty-nine?"

"Excuse me?" I ask, raising an eyebrow. My heart is racing now, and I'm not quite sure if I heard him correctly, though I don't know what else he could've said if that wasn't it.

"I was just asking if you'd ever taken the sixty-nine subway or bus," he says, winking at me and laughing.

"I didn't know there was a sixty-nine subway or bus."

"Oh, I think that must've been in London, then," he says. "Maybe it was one that took me into the West End."

"I wouldn't know," I say, shaking my head.

"Have you ever had a devil's threesome?" he asks. And this time, I know I haven't heard him incorrectly.

"Sorry, what?" My jaw drops. "What did you say?"

"Oh, I'm just joking," he says. "I was just trying to test you to see how you would react if some of these other guys asked you some of these crazy questions."

"Oh, okay. Good test, I guess." I'm not really sure what to say. "So, how's business going?" I ask him, wanting to change the subject.

"As well as can be, considering," he says. "Frannie really wants a mom, you know?" He lowers his voice. "She really wants someone to love her and show her all the girly things that I can't."

"She deserves it," I say, nodding my head. "She is the sweetest girl." And while that's not technically true, I'm not going to add that she really needs a lot more discipline in her life and that he spoils her too much. That is not my place.

"I think she just really needs a mother in her life, you know?"

he says. "But maybe one day we'll find someone as perfect as you to make her pizza and..." I'm very grateful that the bell rings and cuts him off. "Oh, I guess that's time." He frowns, looking disappointed. "Well, I hope your dates continue to go well."

"You too, Danny. I hope you meet someone good," I say, smiling at him. I'm grateful when the night ends. I tick off the box next to Russell's name, hand it in to the people running the event, and look for Isabel.

"So did you like anyone?" she says.

"Yeah, there was one guy who was kind of cute and seemed normal. What about you?"

"There were a couple of guys I thought were fun," she says, nodding. "Let's see if we match."

"Yeah, let's see," I say. We all stand around for what is ten to fifteen minutes, and then the host calls us all to the side and gives us our matches. My eyes are wide and happy when I see that Russell is standing there.

"Hey. You ticked my name, I'm guessing."

"I did. Did you check me?"

"Yeah. You were the only sane one here tonight."

"I guess I won't tell my best friend you said that."

"Oh?" he says, cocking his head to the side. "Why is that?"

"Because she's one of the girls that's here tonight as well."

"Oh." He bursts out laughing. "Then yeah, maybe don't tell her I said that. Which one was she?"

I nod over to Isabel. "Her."

"Oh," he says. "Yeah, she is really pretty. But she was going on about different honeymoon destinations, and I thought that was a weird question, seeing as she had never met any of us before."

"Oh, yeah. That sounds like Isabel. She likes to say controversial things just to see how people react."

"Well, I hope it worked for her," he says. We stand there making small talk, and then Isabel heads over to me.

"I got no matches," she says, shaking her head. "Can you believe it? Not one match."

"I mean, you were talking about honeymoons with the guys."

"I just didn't want anyone to be scared off by the fact that I was looking for marriage," she says, giggling. "I mean, it's not like I'm looking for a one-night stand. I wanted them to know if you match with me, there's a possibility that..." She pauses as she looks over at Russell. "Oh, hey," she says, smiling at him. "You guys matched?" She looks at me in surprise, and I nod.

"Yeah. This is Russell. Russell, this is Isabel."

He says, nodding, "I remember."

I look over at Isabel. "You didn't select him, did you?"

"No." She shakes her head. "He looked aghast when I brought up the honeymoon stuff. I knew he wasn't going to select me back." She grins. "But I don't mind that you guys are a match. Do you want to get out of here and grab a drink somewhere?"

"Sure," I say, looking over at Russell. "That sounds good to me." We head out of the bar and walk down the street until we come to another dive bar at the corner.

"Let's go in here," Isabel says. We walk in, and I immediately groan because I see Sam and Colton standing at the bar. Those are the last two people I want to see.

"Hey, is everything okay?" Russell asks as we step inside. "Your mood immediately changed."

"Oh, it's fine. My brother is just here and..." I pause as Colton walks up to us.

"Hey, how's it going?"

"Hi," I say, glaring at him. "Fancy seeing you here."

"Indeed," he says and holds out his hand. "Hi. I'm Colton Hart. I'm Ella's boss. And you are?"

"Oh, hi. I'm Russell. Ella and I just met at this speed-dating event, and I guess we matched." Russell grins, but Colton just stares at him.

"Oh, interesting," Colton says, looking at Russell and then looking at me. "So, did you guys discuss your last dates and stuff?"

"Yeah," I say, glaring at him, hoping that he's going to keep his mouth shut.

Russell adds on, "Yeah. I think that Ella is really sweet and really honest, and I think that's one of the reasons why we matched."

"Oh, great," Colton says, wrapping his arms around Russell's shoulder, and I don't know if he's doing that to be friendly or trying to intimidate him. "I'm really glad that you're comfortable going on a date with someone who was just banging someone else a couple of days ago." My jaw drops as I stare at Colton. Did he just say what I think he said? I look over at Russell, and I can see that he looks shocked as well.

"Hey, Colton. I think..."

"What?" Colton grins like everything is cool. "Russell, man, I just want to say that you are much better than most other men. I know I wouldn't be comfortable meeting a girl and going to hang out with the guy that she was fucking two days ago. I mean, it's weird, right?" Colton looks over at Russell, and Russell's eyes narrow.

"Sorry, I'm not sure I understand."

"I mean, I was just inside of Ella two days ago," Colton says, winking at me. My jaw drops, and I can feel all the color draining from my face as Colton laughs. "Honey, I'm surprised that you wiped the cum stain off your lips. I felt like you were going to keep it as a souvenir."

"What the fuck?" Russell says as he steps back. He looks at me, and then looks at Colton, and shakes his head. "Hey, dude. Look, I don't know what's going on with you. I didn't know this was your girl." Russell looks over at me. "I thought you were normal."

"I am normal," I say. "Look, please don't listen to him. I..."

"What is going on here? Is this like a joke?" Russell frowns.

Colton shakes his head. "No, everything I said is true." He looks at me. "Ella, did we, or did we not fuck a couple of nights ago?"

I bite down on my lower lip and look at Russell. "Look, it wasn't..."

"Dude, I'm sorry. I'm out of here." Russell turns around and leaves the bar. I can feel fire about to come out of my nostrils as I stare at Colton.

"What the hell do you think you're doing?" I demand. "Why would you say that?"

"What? When he said you'd been honest with him, I just assumed you told him everything."

"Why would I tell him that? It was a speed-dating event. It's not like I'm going to tell him that I slept with someone by mistake, by the way, a few nights ago. I was trying to forget that moment."

"Really?" he says, laughing and running his hands through his hair. "I don't think you were trying to forget anything. I mean, you were..."

"And by the way," I say, cutting him off, "you didn't come on my lips, and there was no cum stain for me to wipe off because I never gave you a blow job, jackass. You wish I did."

He nods slowly and winks again. "You know what? You're right. I would love you to give me a blowy. What about getting down on your knees right now?"

"Are you out of your fricking mind, Colton Hart?" I push past him and head over to Isabel, who is at the bar arguing with Sam. "Isabel, I think we should leave."

"Is everything okay?" she asks, glancing at me. Sam is staring at me and then at Isabel, and I have no idea what is going on. Colton comes up behind me and puts his hand on my shoulder. I push it off and stare at him through narrowed eyes.

"You are a jackass."

"Excuse me, what did you say?" He looks over at Sam. "Sam, what did your sister just say to me?"

Sam looks at me and then looks at Colton and shakes his head. "I'm not sure. What did you just say, Ella?"

"Nothing," I say through gritted teeth. I know I can't let my brother know how pissed off I am because then he might want to know why. And the last thing I want him to know is that I hooked up with his best friend a couple of nights ago. I grab Colton by the arm and pull him down the bar so we're out of Sam's earshot. "Listen to me and listen to me again. We are never going to fuck again," I say. "I'm never going to give you a blow job and…" I feel his hand on my hip, wrapping around my waist, and my body trembles. "What are you doing?"

"What do you think I'm doing?" he asks, winking. He leans forward, his lips near my ear and whispers, "I know you want me, Ella. I know your panties are wet right now. I know you wish we were somewhere else other than here so that you could bounce up and down on my hard cock. I know how badly you want me inside of you right now." I listen to his words, and while I can't deny them, I'm pissed off, even though my body wants him, my brain thinks he is the biggest asshole. I stare at him for a couple of seconds, and I'm about to go off on him. I'm about to tell him to keep his job, to keep his money and to get a life, but then a little devil inside of me decides that I should play his game.

I stare at him for a couple of seconds, knowing that he is expecting me to go off. He thinks he's got the better of me, but I'm not going to let that happen. I place my hand on his chest and look up at him with wide, innocent eyes. "Well, you might just be a little bit right. You want to get out of here, Colton?" I ask, running my fingers down toward the top of his pants. "Or do you think you need to stay here and hang out with Sam?"

10

Colton stares at me as if he's not quite sure what I've just said. I can tell that he's intrigued but not trusting me. I look over my shoulder to make sure my brother isn't watching, and I slip my fingers farther down the front of his pants and rub gently. I can feel that he's already hard, so I squeeze him a little bit. He growls and grabs my hand.

"Don't play around unless you're ready to get dirty," he says, and I giggle slightly.

I bite down on my lip and stare at his lips.

"Oh, I'm more than ready to get dirty," I say. "I'm ready to get..." I pause because I can't think of the right word, and he leans forward.

"Are you ready to get wet?"

"Oh, honey, I'm already wet," I say, cringing slightly and sighing but loving the way he's reacting to my words.

Why is it always so easy with men? It isn't because he's super cocky that he believes that I'm just going to forgive and forget how much of an asshole he is, and not less than ten minutes ago.

"So you want to go back to my place?" he says.

"I don't know if I can wait that long," I say, pouting. I press my breasts into his chest. "I feel like I need you now."

"Fuck, you are so hot, Ella," he says. He looks over at Sam, then grabs my hand. "Come on." He pulls me to the front of the bar, and then we go down a side hallway.

"Get in there," he says and pushes me into the bathroom.

I stare at him in surprise, though I shouldn't really be. Did I expect him to take me to a five-star hotel? No, that is not how Colton Hart operates.

"I knew you wanted me, baby," he says as he presses his lips against mine.

I kiss him back passionately, loving the feel of his lips against mine as we tumble around in the dark bathroom. I try not to look at my surroundings too much or smell because it's totally not a sexy place to be, but I'm so hot and horny I don't even care. I know that I need to tease him. I know that I need to make him frustrated, so I decide to just go with it. I kiss him back, and I don't stop his fingers when they run up the inside of my top and slip under my bra. I moan against his lips as his fingers pinch my nipples.

There's a banging on the door, and we both freeze for a couple of seconds.

"Who's in there?" a deep voice sounds. "I need to go."

"I might be in here a while, man," Colton says loudly. "I have the shits," he says again, and I roll my eyes as he winks.

"What were we doing?" he says as he turns back to me, and we start kissing again.

It's hot, and it's sexy, and it's primal, and if I didn't think he was an absolute jackass, I would definitely go all the way. I can barely think. Every nerve ending in my body is turned on, and I love the way he makes me feel when he reaches and pulls my top off. I don't stop him, and when he undoes my bra and places it in the sink, I don't stop him. He grabs me around the waist and lifts me up, and I wrap my arms around his neck as he positions me on the counter.

"I hope this doesn't break," I say.

"You're not that heavy," he says, chuckling, and I just roll my eyes at him.

I start undoing the buttons on his shirt and run my fingers down his bare skin. He's hot, and I can feel his heart racing. He leans me back slightly, and his lips go to my nipple and start sucking. I close my eyes. I've never felt so turned on before in my life. I reach over, undo his button and unzip him. He pushes his pants down slightly. I stare at his large cock, purple and proud, the veins pulsing, and I lick my lips.

"You want to suck?" he says, and I press my finger to his lips for a couple of seconds.

"Maybe afterward," I lie, knowing there's no way I'm going to suck him tonight.

He grabs my waist and pulls me forward slightly, then reaches his hands up under my skirt and pulls down my panties. I moan slightly as he pulls them off my legs completely and then sniffs them.

"These smell fucking hot," he says, stuffing my panties in his jeans pocket. "I'll keep these, I think."

I just stare at him, my heart racing. I cannot believe what we're doing. A part of me thinks that this is a mistake. A part of me thinks that if we get caught, I'm going to be in even bigger trouble than I was before. It's one thing to be found in his apartment the day after; it's another thing to be fucking in a seedy bathroom of a club. My brother will kill me, and my parents will disown me.

He runs his fingers down between the valley of my breasts and then grabs his cock. He rubs the head against my slit, and I moan slightly.

"Are you trying to get me pregnant or something?"

He growls as he continues to rub my clit, and I flick my hair back. He leans forward and kisses me again. It's hot and heavy, and I want nothing more than for him to be inside of me.

"Fuck," he whispers against my lips. "I don't even have any condoms," he groans and I feel his disappointment twisting inside of me. "You and those stupid balloons."

"Oh, man," I say, looking at him with a sad face. "Shucks, I forgot about that."

"I can pull out, though," he says, his cock between my legs, ready to thrust inside of me. I want him inside of me so badly, but instead, I push him away.

"I don't think so," I say. "You're my boss. It wouldn't really be appropriate to get pregnant by my boss. Do you know how that would look?" I say, biting down on my lower lip as I quickly grab my bra and top and put them back on. I pull my skirt down and watch as he stares at me with a confused expression on his face.

"Wait, what?" he rubs his forehead and frowns. I hate that the look makes my heart leap. "What are you doing?"

"I'm getting dressed so I can get out of here."

"Oh, are we going to go back to my place?" he says, staring at me as he does the buttons of his shirt back up. "We can pick up some rubbers on the way."

"I don't think so, Colton," I say coldly as I grab a piece of toilet paper and wipe it against his face. "You have lipstick on your cheek," I explain, smiling sweetly. "I don't want Sam to ask you where it came from."

"Where are you going?" he says as I walk to the door and look back at him.

"I'm going to go and get Isabel, and we're going to go and grab a pizza or something, and I'm going home, and who knows? Maybe, just maybe, I'll find Russell's number and tell him exactly what's going on, or maybe I'll invite—"

"That dude is not going to be going over to your place," he says, "knowing I was inside of you a couple of days ago."

"Well, you might have ruined that connection, but

you're not going to ruin the next one that I make, Colton. Trust me."

"So what? You're just going to leave me here with blue balls?"

I grin wickedly at his question. That was the plan.

11

"Oh my gosh, that man absolutely infuriates me," I say to Isabel as we make our way back to my place. "I can't stand him."

"Really?" Isabel says, looking over at me.

"What do you mean, 'Really?'" I glare at her, still feeling hot and bothered from my encounter with Colton.

"I just feel like you guys have chemistry, which you don't want to acknowledge."

"I have acknowledged it."

"Well, is sleeping with him acknowledging it, or just—"

"Really, Isabel? I am so pissed right now. He is so full of himself. He destroyed—"

"Hold on a second." Isabel holds her hand up. "He didn't destroy anything."

"He destroyed my relationship with Russell."

"Girl, you barely knew that man. You don't even know his last name," she says, and I pause. "I'm sorry. You know, I know that you and Colton have a history, but he might be better now."

"He's not better now. He fired me after one hour when I

first started working for him, and now he's ruined a potentially great relationship."

I hold my hand up and stare at her as we get to my door. "Do not say that Russell and I didn't have a relationship."

"Well, you didn't," she says sarcastically. I can tell she's annoyed, and I wonder if it has to do with me or what she was arguing with Sam about in the bar.

"I mean a potential. We both connected."

"He most probably thought you looked hot and wanted to try and hook up with you," she says, "because you do look hot."

"Well, thank you. I guess I will take that as a compliment." I sigh. "I think Colton thought I looked hot, too."

"Well, didn't you say you almost banged him in the bathroom?" She shakes her head as we make our way up the stairs toward my apartment. "Which I think is crazy, by the way. You banged him once, and now you almost banged him again."

"Do we have to say 'bang,' Isabel? That's so crude."

"I mean, it was kind of crude. You were in a dirty-ass bathroom. He has your panties in his pocket. Come on, Ella. It's not like you're some shy virgin who's never had sex before. You literally had a one-night stand with a guy, and you almost had a two-night stand tonight."

"I told you that was part of my plan. I was going to tease him and turn him on and then leave him with blue balls."

"Yeah, but you left yourself horny, too."

"I don't want to talk about it."

"So why did he fire you again?" she asks me as we make our way into the apartment with the steaming hot cheese-and-pepperoni pizza.

"Honestly, I don't really know."

I look over at her as we make our way to the living room and sit down. I turn on the TV for background noise while she opens the box, and we both reach in and grab a slice. "Tell me again what happened?"

"I mean, not really much happened. I was only there one hour. I was in his office, and he basically told me that he was going to start the official training after he had a meeting. And this older guy comes in, some billionaire that was his mentor, and was speaking to me and asking me where I went to school and if I was dating anyone. And I said no. And then he says, and I'm pretty sure he was joking, 'Oh, have you ever thought about being a sugar baby?' And I replied because I was joking as well, 'Oh, no. Why? What does that entail?' Anyway, that was it. I didn't say yes or anything. The billionaire, I can't even remember his name now, goes into the office, and ten minutes later, Colton comes out, walks over to my desk, and says, 'You're fired.' My jaw dropped. I was like, 'What?' He's like, 'Please leave now. You're fired.'"

"Oh my gosh, Ella." Isabel looks at me with wide eyes. "Do you think he thought you were coming on to his mentor?"

"What? No. Why would he think that?"

"You said you were joking around about being a sugar baby."

"Yeah, but I was joking. Of course I wasn't interested in being some old dude's sugar baby."

"But does Colton know that?"

"I mean, I shouldn't have to specifically tell him that. I'm not that sort of girl. He's been best friends with Sam for ages. He's known me. That's why I got the job."

"Yeah, but he didn't really know you that well, right?"

"What do you mean?"

"I mean, you were in school. I'm sure you weren't hanging out with him and Sam fairly often."

"I guess that's true."

"So do you think he thinks that?"

"I don't know," I say. "If that's what he thought, then he should have said something to me. Anyway, I'm just so annoyed by him."

"Well, why don't you just quit?"

"I can't quit. If I quit, my parents will kill me and be so disappointed, and Sam will be disappointed. And I need the money, Isabel. I have bills to pay."

"I know. What about if you make him fire you again?"

"What? What do you mean?"

"If he fires you, maybe he'll give you a severance package and you can say, 'Oh, is this sexual harassment?'"

"Oh my gosh, what?"

"I'm just saying, if you get him to fire you, then you can't take the blame. And maybe he'll keep his mouth shut about what really went on."

"I guess, but how am I going to make him fire me?"

"Maybe you can join a dating app and bring all your dates around him and pretend that you're looking for a sugar daddy, seeing as he thought you were in the first place."

"I don't know about that," I say. "It doesn't seem like the best idea."

"Well, it might not be the best idea, but it's an idea. He obviously wasn't happy when he saw you with Russell, so he's probably not going to be happy if he sees you with all these other guys."

"That's true. Fine, I will do it." I am not sure this is the best idea in the world, but it's not like I have a history with good ideas, anyway. I know that this is the worst reasoning in the world, but I'm too tired to call myself out. "We can sign up, but I'm not going to go on any dates with any losers."

"Honey, most of the guys on those apps are losers, and you just don't even realize it until you're on the date with them."

"I guess," I say, looking over at her. "Is this a bad idea?"

"I don't know. Do you even know what he wants from you?"

"What do you mean, what he wants from me?"

"Look, you had a one-night stand with Colton, right?"

"Yeah."

"You enjoyed it?"

"It was okay, but he obviously enjoyed it. I guess so."

"Your brother shows up and then you lie and you say you're Colton's assistant, and he doesn't dismiss that."

"Yeah, because he didn't want Sam to know."

"Okay, for whatever reason, he doesn't dismiss it. But now he actually wants you to work for him."

"Yeah. And?"

"So why?" She looks at me. "Have you ever thought about that?"

"No," I say, shaking my head. "I have no idea why."

"Well, it's probably because he wants to fuck you all over his office, girl. Most probably, he had a piece of you, and he wants to have as much of you as he can until he no longer wants you."

"Thanks, Isabel. That makes me feel really amazing."

"I'm just saying. You know guys like that."

"No, actually, I don't really know guys like that. He's the only billionaire I know."

"You know what I mean."

"I guess."

"Anyway, play his game. He thinks he's in control. Well, you showed him tonight, 'I can have you or not have you. I don't care.' Let him know, 'Just because you're rich and hot doesn't mean you're the only guy that I can get. I can get other guys.'"

"But I can't get other guys."

"That's why you're going to go on the dating app. Duh."

"Okay, I guess. Why do I feel like this is not going to go well for me?"

"Trust me, Ella," she says with a grin. "It's going to go perfectly."

I should have known then that everything was going to go the opposite of perfectly.

12

Two boring days later, I find myself at the ice cream store buying two pints of ice cream. Whenever I feel anxious or nervous, I always resort to ice cream. And while I love Häagen-Dazs and Ben & Jerry's, Sweet Sprinkles has the best ice cream in New York City. And now that I have a job that is paying me well, I want to treat myself. I know that Isabel's idea isn't the best, but I am one of those people who always seems to get suckered into bad ideas.

The point of the matter is that Colton really hurt and embarrassed me when he fired me so many years ago. And even though I enjoyed hooking up with him, I hate him thinking that he can have me whenever he wants. I hate him knowing just how much I enjoyed the night with him. It was hot, and he was hot, and in any other circumstance, I wouldn't feel bad about hooking up with a virtual stranger. I'm not a prude, though it isn't like I go around having one-night stands. I am annoyed with myself because I still continued to sleep with Colton once I figured it out. Because no part of me has ever been able to turn away at that moment. I want to show him that even though he thinks he is the bee's knees, I can still do better, get better, and not have to put up with him. I don't really want to go through a bunch of old rich men to make a point, but it is what it is.

I look at the text messages on my phone. Colton has messaged me asking me to come to his office. He wants to go over a schedule for the next week. I haven't responded yet because I am annoyed and frankly slightly nervous about what it will mean to actually work with him in an office again. I nearly had sex with him in a dirty bathroom. Will I be able to resist him in an office?

"Oh my gosh. It's Ella." I hear Frannie's voice, and I turn around in surprise. Frannie and Danny are walking into the ice cream store.

"Hey," I say, waving.

"Daddy asked me if I wanted to get ice cream," she says. "And you're here." She grabs my hand. "I'm so happy to see you, Ella."

"I'm always happy to see you, Frannie," I say. I look over at Danny, and he's grinning at me. "Hey," I say. "Fancy seeing you here."

"I know," he says. "We must stop meeting like this." He gives me a small smile. "How did the dating stuff go?"

"You know, It didn't go very well. What about for you?"

"Well," he says, "there was one lady I had my eye on, but I'm not sure if she's interested." He shrugs. "But you never know."

"Oh?" I say. "Did you mark her name off?"

"No." He shakes his head. "I was pretty sure she wasn't going to mark my name off."

"Oh no. Why is that?"

"I think she thinks it would be too complicated to date me."

"Oh?" My heart starts pounding then because I'm slightly nervous that he's talking about me. But he can't be talking about me, can he? I am his much younger babysitter.

And sure, lots of younger women hit it off with older men, and he isn't that much older, but I thought I made it pretty clear I am not interested in him.

"So, what are you up to this evening?" he asks as I stare at him awkwardly.

"Oh, I think I'm just going to watch some TV and..."

"Do you think I could ask you a huge favor?"

"Sure. What is it?" I ask him.

"I have to do some work this evening, and I really need someone to look after Frannie."

"Oh," I say, wishing I didn't say that I don't have much going on. "Are you working at home or..."

"No, I'll be out of the house." He sighs. "I know this is really late notice, and I hate to do this to you, but do you think you could possibly look after Frannie? I'll pay you double time."

"Oh," I say. "I mean, you don't have to do that. That's a really generous offer, but I did get a new job and..."

"And what?" he asks.

"I'm supposed to go into the office tomorrow for a meeting with my new boss, but..."

"But what?" he says.

"I mean, I guess I can do this for you. I really appreciate you giving me work," I say, looking down at Frannie, not knowing how I can say no to her.

"Perfect," he says. "Shall we get the ice cream and then just go back to my place?"

"Sure," I say, nodding. "Sounds good."

"Yay. I'm going to be with Ella. I'm going to be with Ella." Frannie lets go of my hand and start skipping around the room. "I love you, Ella," she says, beaming at me. "I wish you were my mommy."

"Aw," I say, feeling slightly hot. "Well, I'm sure you'll have a mommy soon," I mumble and look over at Danny. "I hope it goes well."

"I hope so as well." His eyes are on me, and there's a weird glint as he looks me up and down. I know I need to speak to Isabel. I need to ask her what she thinks. I may be overthinking it. I may be going crazy. There's no way he's interested in me. He's never really said or done anything to make me think that he is. "Great, Ella," he says. "Is there anything else you want here to go?"

"No, I'm good. Thank you." I smile at him, and he pulls out his wallet and withdraws a stack of twenty-dollar bills. I'm glad it's not dollar bills, or he would have made me feel like a stripper.

"Let me give this to you now," he says, beaming as he hands me stacks of money. I almost wait for him to make a comment about making it rain, and I chastise myself internally.

"Oh, you don't..."

"No, it's fine," he says. "Frannie loves you, and we've come to depend upon you. I'm really grateful that you would take the job at the last moment. I'm really grateful for all the moments you've come over and looked after us," he says. "You're special, Ella."

"Thank you," I say, smiling, happy that someone recognizes that I'm a good person. "You're a really good dad, Danny, and I really hope that you find someone who will be Frannie's mom so you don't have to hire me anymore." I try to emphasize the "hire me anymore" because I don't want him to think I want the role, but I can't tell if he's taken it the right way or not. He's just looking at me with a dreamy expression, and all of a sudden I'm feeling like everything in my life is getting way too complicated.

13

"Okay. It's time for bed, Frannie," I say, escorting the girl to her small room. "It's time for you to go to sleep."

"But I don't want to go to sleep. I want to wait up for Daddy," she says, pouting, looking at me with big, beguiling eyes that make me want to pull her into my arms and hug her.

"Well, it's seven o'clock, and it's past your bedtime," I say. "I think you'll just have to wait until tomorrow morning."

"But I can't say good night to Daddy in the morning. That will be morning. I'll say, 'Good morning, Daddy.'"

"That's true," I say, laughing, knowing that the little girl has stumped me. "Frannie"—I look at my watch—"you know that if you want pancakes for breakfast..."

"Are you going to make them, Ella? Yes. You make the most delicious pancakes ever."

"Well, I most probably won't be here in the morning because I'll go home once your daddy gets back."

"Why don't you ever stay like Daddy's other friends?"

I stare at her for a few seconds, not sure how to answer that. "Um, I think your daddy's other friends are most probably special friends if they're staying over," I say quickly, not wanting to hear about Danny's live-in lovers or friends with benefits.

"Daddy says you're his favorite special friend," she says, beaming at me. "He says that you are the sort of woman that every man wants to marry and fall in love with because you're perfect. And you're the best babysitter I ever had, and I love you, Ella," she says, opening up her arms wide.

I give her a huge cuddle and rub the top of her hair. "Want me to read you a story before bedtime?"

"No," she says, shaking her head. "I think I'll just go to sleep. That way, I'll wake up faster and then I get to see Daddy faster."

"That is true," I say, and my phone starts ringing. I look at the screen and see that it's Isabel.

"You can take that if you want, Ella. I'm just going to brush my teeth and then go to bed."

"Okay. Are you sure?"

"Yes."

"Well, you come out to the living room if you need anything, okay, Frannie?"

"Yes, I will," she says as I answer the phone and head out of the bedroom.

"Hey, chica, what's going on?"

"Not much."

"How's the dating app?"

"Ugh," I groan. "I deleted that shit already. It was annoying me. I already got three dick pics and a bunch of messages at one o'clock in the morning about, 'What are you doing?' And I'm like, 'What do you think I'm doing? I'm in bed sleeping.'"

"You know what they wanted," she says, laughing.

"Yeah, I know what they wanted and you know what they wanted, and they were not about to get that from me."

"I guess only Colton can get that from you, huh?"

"Very funny, Isabel. I'm not trying to find a fuckboy just because I want Colton to think I'm not into him."

"You want him to think that, or you're not interested?" she says.

"You know what I mean. I'm not interested," I say quickly. "Anyway, the app is done."

"I had a feeling you might do that," she says, "but I have an even better idea."

"Oh, boy. Why does that make me nervous?"

"What do you mean? Why are you nervous?"

"All your good ideas make me nervous because they never really seem to be good for me."

"That's because you never execute them properly. If you execute them exactly as I say, it will..."

"Isabel, don't even get me started," I say as she giggles.

"But trust me, this one is perfect."

"How so?"

"You ever heard of sugarbabiez.com?"

"Sugar babies?" I repeat. "Like Jelly Babies?"

"No, sugarbabiez with a Z."

"How was I meant to know it had a *Z* and not an *S*?" I say.

"I was trying to pronounce the *Z*."

"What do you mean, sugarbabiez.com? You're going to have to explain to me what it is if it's not candy."

"Okay. So it's a site for young women who want to meet older men who want to take care of them, like sugar daddies."

"Isabel, are you telling me that you think I should sign up for a website to find a sugar daddy?"

"No. Calm down. Of course not."

"So then, why are you bringing it up?"

"Because you're totally going to sign up."

"You just said..."

"You're not going to sign up because that's what you really want, goofy." She laughs. "You're going to sign up because we're pretty sure that Colton fired you because you were trying to make his mentor your sugar daddy, right?"

"But I wasn't trying to do that! I..."

"It doesn't matter if you were or if you weren't. He obviously got it into his head that that was something you were interested in."

"Okay, and how does this help? It will just reinforce the fact that he thinks I'm interested in it."

"Exactly. He wanted to be a jackass to you before. Well, let him have a reason to be a jackass."

"What are you saying?"

"Pretend you're looking for a sugar daddy, girl. He has to know that you aren't really looking for a sugar daddy because he's not that dumb. He's rich for a reason. So obviously, he was doing that to be a jackass to you. So let's pretend that maybe now you've changed your personality and you are looking for a sugar daddy. He is going to go out of his mind when he thinks you left him for a sugar daddy."

"Um, I can't leave him if I'm not with him."

"You know what I mean," she says, giggling. "He still wants to hook up with you, right?"

"I mean, I guess. You know men love those situations where they can just hook up as much as they want."

"Exactly. He wants to hook up with you. Sure, he might not want a relationship with you, but even if he doesn't want a relationship with you, he will get possessive and territorial. Pretend that you've got another man, a sugar daddy, and you don't need him."

"I don't know, Isabel. This sounds awfully complicated.

And how the hell am I meant to let him know that I have a sugar daddy? It's not like I'm going to tell Sam and he's going to pass on the information. My parents would ship me back to Florida before we could blink if they thought I was even thinking about such a thing."

"You just sign up, start messaging with people, and leave your profile open around him. You know men are nosy. He's going to look."

"Oh, I guess. Let me think about it."

"Trust me," she says, laughing. "He is going to go out of his mind if you do such a thing."

My phone beeps, and I look at the screen and see that Colton is calling me. I groan. "Well, speak of the devil."

"What?" she says. "A sugar daddy already?"

"Isabel, really? How is a sugar daddy already contacting me if I'm not even on the website yet?"

"Oh, yeah." She laughs. "What's going on?"

"Colton's on the other line. I will call you back in a second."

"Okay. But promise me one thing."

"What?"

"Don't have phone sex."

I hang up the phone instead of answering her. "Yeah, can I help you, Colton?" I snap into the phone, not wanting him to think that I want to talk to him.

"Hey. Yeah. My company is breaking ground on a new residential real estate deal in New Jersey and Pennsylvania, and we're also developing something in Southwest Florida in the Sarasota area. I'm going to need you to figure out the estimated property taxes for each parcel based on the information we give you for each house."

"What?" I say, staring into the phone, wondering if I heard him correctly.

"Yeah. You're my assistant, and I'm paying you a lot of

money, so I'm going to need you to come into the office tomorrow and work on this."

"Are you out of your mind?" I say. "That is not even in my wheelhouse. That is..."

"I guess you're going to have to figure out how to do it, aren't you?"

I bite down on my lip. "You know what? Sure. I'll be in the office tomorrow, bright and early."

"Good," he smirks as if there could have been no other reasonable answer. "And I mean, if you want to come over..."

"Excuse me?" I am not even entertaining that thought. "I don't think so."

"Think about it..." He pauses, and the screen flashes. FaceTime is on the screen, and I reluctantly hit accept.

"Why are you FaceTiming me?" I glare at the screen, trying to ignore the way his face is both boyish and rugged. He's grinning at me like he's about to tell me the funniest joke in the world and I can't help but soften my own expression.

"Because I was hoping you were naked," he says, grinning into the phone.

I stare at his handsome face and roll my eyes. "Well, I wouldn't answer the phone if I was naked."

"But you can get naked now if you want to."

"I don't want to, Colton. I definitely do not want to get naked. Just in case you're not clear, I don't want you either. I don't want you whatsoever."

"Maybe one of these days those words will be true, but they sure are not true now," he says, laughing. "Ms. Soaking Panties."

"Excuse me?" I gasp at his last words to me. Had he really just said what I thought I heard?

"I know your panties are wet," he says, winking. His blue eyes twinkle and remind me of the stars on a dark night in Florida. They beckon to me, and I wonder what's going through his head. I feel a sense of surrealism as I sit there, processing the situation as it's happening.

"No, they're not. You wish."

"I don't need to wish," he says confidently, and I try not to squirm because, of course, he's right. "I bet you a thousand dollars."

"Okay, you're on. A thousand dollars it is. Easy money for me."

"You don't even know how I'm going to confirm, though."

"I know they're not wet, so it doesn't matter," I say nonchalantly, sitting back. I almost forget that I'm not at home.

"Okay. So for a thousand dollars we have to figure it out?"

"Yes," I say, my mind thinking this is going to be the easiest thousand dollars I ever make in my life.

"Take off your panties right now," he says, leaning forward like he wants to jump through the screen.

"What?" My jaw drops in shock. Is he out of his mind? Who would ever take their panties off during a video chat? I mean, asides from porno stars. And I am certainly not a porno star.

"Take off your panties right now and show them to me. If I can see moisture on them, it means they're wet. If they look dry, you win a thousand dollars."

"I'm not taking off my panties right now." I scoff as if he's crazy. "You just want me to flash you."

"I'm not telling you to put your phone camera all up in your pussy," he says the words slowly and deliberately and I blush. "I don't need to see that right now." He licks his lips like that's the treat that will come later.

"Right now?" I stare at the screen. "Are you out of your mind? You're not seeing it right now, in five minutes or in five decades. It's not happening, Colton."

"It's a thousand dollars. I can deduct it from your paycheck or..."

"You know what? Hold on," I say, placing the phone down on the couch. I quickly jump up, pull off my panties, and stare at them. I bite down on my lip. They're soaking wet, not as wet as they could have been, but pretty clearly wet. I wonder if that will show on the screen. I grab a glass of water and the phone and stare at him. "Hey," I say, drinking the water.

"Are you going to show me your panties?"

"Yeah. They're not wet, like I said." I hold the panties in my fingers in front of the phone, feeling slightly embarrassed.

"I can't see the crotch area."

"You're disgusting. I'm not going..." I pause as I hear the door opening. "Oh, shit. I've got to go," I say and close the phone down and put the phone and the glass of water back down on the coffee table. I hear Danny coming in, and I look around for somewhere to put my panties. I stuff them into the side of the couch quickly, hoping that he doesn't see them and reminding myself to remember to pick them up before I leave.

"Hey," Danny says, stretching. "Good to see you."

"You too. You're back earlier than I thought you would be. Frannie just brushed her teeth and went to bed."

"Oh, that's good," he says, nodding. "I'm actually not going to be here for very long. I have to get up early. So I was wondering if you would stay the night."

"Oh, but I have to go to my job tomorrow."

"I promise I'll be back by six."

"I don't know. I..."

"You can take my bed," he offers, walking over to me. "And I'll sleep on the couch."

"Okay," I say, sighing. I don't really know how to say no if he has to go back out to work. "But please be back by six because I need to go home and shower and change and then be at the office by, like, eight."

"I got you," he says, smiling. "So you want to watch a movie? Or..."

"No, I should just head to the room and lie down," I say, feeling slightly awkward. "Maybe I'll have a shower."

"Okay. You know where the towels are," he says.

I head toward the bedroom and close it behind me. I really don't want to stay here, especially not in Danny's room. I sit on the edge of the bed and stare at my phone, wondering what I'm going to do. I have five text messages from Colton with smiley faces and two comments stating, "You owe me a thousand dollars." He most probably thinks I hung up because I didn't want to show him my panties, but I freeze as I realize that my panties are still on the couch.

"Fuck," I whisper under my breath. A slight knocking on the door makes me jump up. "You can come in," I say, looking over at the doorway as Danny comes in. There's a wide smirk on his face.

"Hey, I think you forgot these." My panties are in his hand, and he throws them to me. There's a look on his face that makes me want to crawl under a rock and die. This has to be one of the most embarrassing moments in my life. I am not sure if I will ever recover from this moment.

"Oh, I spilled water on them," I say quickly, groaning inside as I realize how stupid I sound. How the hell does one spill water on their panties? Worst lie ever.

"It's okay," he says, laughing. "Hey, if you ever spill water on them again and you need help drying them, I can help." He licks his tongue across his lips and winks at me, and I can feel myself blushing. "I'm just joking," he says quickly. "You have a good night now."

"Thanks. You too," I say. Because how else do you respond to that? It's not like I can tell him he's being inappropriate. I could imagine going in front of a judge and pleading my case. "Well, your honor, I do admit that my panties were on his couch, yes, but he was the one that was out of line for waggling his tongue at me. Yeah, the judge would have lots of sympathy for me. Not.

He closes the door behind him, and I know that there is something definitely wrong in this situation. I don't know what is going on, but I really hope Danny doesn't think that I left the panties for him to find.

14

I feel like I am doing the walk of shame as I make my way into the office the next morning. I try hard not to think about Danny and the events of the previous evening. I feel like I am living in a nightmare where, every day, I find myself in even more awful and precarious positions. I try not to think of Danny's flirtatious face this morning when I was leaving. His sly comment asking if I left any presents for him in his room made my skin crawl. I wasn't sure if he was joking or serious, but I really hoped that he didn't think I left him my panties on purpose last night because that was definitely not the case.

I really hope that Colton is not going to be there this morning. I don't want to see him. I don't want to talk about our phone call. I especially don't want him to talk about any of our intimate moments. There have been far too many of them. I don't know why I can't seem to resist him. And I don't really want to analyze the reasons why he sets my skin on fire.

It's not like he's utterly gorgeous.

Or that his soulful blue eyes seem to pierce my soul.

His perfectly coiffed, silky golden-brown hair doesn't feel like heaven on my fingers.

And his abs for days don't make my stomach flip.

I certainly didn't wake up this morning thinking about his smirk and how it sends my entire body racing for cover.

I am not interested in him.

Whatsoever.

I really hope he's not going to be there this morning. I just want one day to just be and relax.

The office is busy this morning. I'm not sure if that is normal as I haven't been here in years, but I sure hope that the long line of people isn't going to make me late. I know that there is a one-hundred-percent certainty that if I'm late, Colton will be there. Just waiting for me with that devious, "I'm better than you" look on his face.

I try not to sigh as I join the line. There are at least five other people standing by reception waiting to check in. I attempt to brush my hair back with my fingers as I wait. I'd forgotten to put it up due to my rushing to get away from Danny, and I knew it had to look a frizzy mess.

My phone beeps and I look at the screen, expecting to see Colton's name, but it's not him. It's one of my good friends, Sarah. I answer quickly.

"Hey girl, I can't talk long. I'm at work."

"Work?" She sounds surprised and I realize I haven't updated her on any of my recent shenanigans. "Yay, I'm so glad you got a job." She sounds pleased for me because she knows the state of my finances just as well as Isabel does.

"Oh, it's not even a real job," I say in hushed tones. "You don't even want to know what drama I've gotten myself into."

"Ooh, do tell." She giggles. "I need some excitement in my life. Is it super dramatic?"

"Really, Sarah?"

"Sorry, but you can't just leave me hanging. How do you get a job that isn't really a real job? And does it pay?"

"It pays, but it's not like I even applied for it."

"You got a job you didn't apply for? How?"

"I slept with the boss," I say darkly and I smile when I hear her gasp in shock. I really shouldn't be enjoying telling the story so much. It's not like it makes me look good.

"What is this new job? You're not a stripper, are you?"

"No, I am not a stripper. What do you and Isabel think of me?" I moan, wondering why both of my friends assumed I would become a stripper or an escort. "I'm working for a large corporation as an assistant."

"You what?"

"To the CEO."

"Damn, girl, you slept with an old man?"

"Colton is not an old man."

"Colton." She pauses. "Colton Hart? Sam's best friend?"

"Yeah, maybe." I don't really want to admit that, but I guess I don't have a choice. His name isn't that common.

"Wait, didn't you work for him before and he fired your ass on the same day you started?"

"Don't remind me."

"You slept with him?"

"Like I said, don't remind me."

"Girl, I need the tea."

"I will tell you later. Hold on a sec." I put my phone down next to my stomach and smile at the blonde receptionist. "Hello, today is my first day. I'm Colton Hart's new assistant."

"Oh, you must be Ella Wynter." She grabs a badge and hands it to me. Her eyes flicker up and down my attire and I can tell she's not impressed. "This is a temporary badge to get you into the elevators and up to the tenth floor, where you'll be working with Mr. Hart. You will have to go to HR to get an official badge sometime this week. They will take a photo, so you might want to do your hair and some makeup."

I try not to blush at her comment. I was sure she must have been wondering how I was able to get this job. I wasn't going to be stupid enough to tell her.

"Thank you," I say, taking the temporary badge and heading toward the elevator. I feel like a fraud. I have no idea what I'm really meant to be doing and pessimistic thoughts of when I worked for Colton previously flash into my mind.

I get into the elevator and I look around. There's no one else in here with me and I'm grateful for that. I need to gather my thoughts. I press the button to take me to the tenth floor and stand there quite impatiently. I'm feeling slightly nervous. I'm slightly overwhelmed by the events of the last forty-eight hours. Everything in my life seems to be going crazy and I don't know if that's a good thing or a bad thing. I had been complaining to Isabel and Sarah about how monotonous my life was just a few months ago, but I didn't think I wanted this much excitement.

The elevator pinged and I walked out and looked around. I had no idea where I was going. I see a handsome young man sitting at a desk to the right and I walk over to him.

"Hi," I say, smiling widely. "I am here to work for..."

"Oh, you must be Colton's new assistant," he cut me off and stood up cheerfully. "We've been waiting on you. Nice to meet you. I'm Adam."

"Hi, Adam. Nice to meet you. I'm Ella."

"Great. Let me take you through. Colton said that as soon as you arrived, I was to show you to his office."

"Oh, awesome," I say, nodding. I'm surprised that Colton had told people in the office about me, seeing as how unconventional the job was.

I follow Adam down a small hallway and then he stops and knocks on the door.

"Come in," I hear Colton's voice barking.

Adam opens the door and steps in.

"Hey, Colton. Your new assistant, Ella, is here."

I step in behind him and stare at Colton. He's sitting behind one of the largest cherry oak desks I've ever seen in my life. There are stacks of files on one side. He nods. "Thank you, Adam."

"Ella, you may have a seat," he says to me, and I walk over to the chair.

"Adam," he says as Adam leaves.

"Yes, sir?"

"Close the door behind you."

"Yes, sir."

Adam closes the door and I feel like I've somehow entered a jail cell. I take a seat in the leather chair and look into Colton's laughing blue eyes.

"Good morning," I say after a couple of minutes of silence.

"What time do you think this is?" he says, looking at his watch. His eyes narrow as he looks me up and down. "And are you wearing the same clothes I saw you in last night?"

I press my lips together. "What are you talking about?"

"Yesterday, when we FaceTimed, you were wearing those clothes. You didn't change?"

He leans back and I can see that he's thinking hard.

"I didn't change because I didn't go home," I say softly.

He leans forward, his hands together. "So you hooked up then."

"That's not what I'm saying."

"I'm saying that you hooked up with your kid's dad."

"Well, number one, she's not my kid. If she was my kid, I wouldn't be babysitting. And her father Danny had to work. In fact, you got me into a lot of trouble yesterday."

"I did?" he looks baffled. "How is that?"

"When you told me to take my panties off," I whisper.

And he starts chuckling like that's a fun memory in his mind. Which it most probably was. I would bet $5 that he had a fantasy of me stripping my panties off for him.

"And what happened to those *wet* panties?" He's enjoying this far too much for my liking.

"Let's just say Danny found them. He thought I left them for him on purpose."

He shakes his head and starts laughing. "I expect that you're not going to work for him any longer?"

"Well, you expect incorrectly. I have been helping him out for a long time and I will continue to help him out because that's what he needs of me. His daughter doesn't have a mom and..."

"Oh, and you're trying out for the position?" he says.

"No, I'm not trying out for the position. There is no position. I've just been working for him for a while and he trusts me. And Frannie..."

Colton held his hands up. "Tell someone who cares," he says. "Look, Ella, I'm going to need you to take this a lot more seriously and be a lot more professional."

"What?" I say, my jaw dropping as I stare at him.

"I've given you a job here and..."

"You didn't give me a job because I actually wanted to work for you. It's not like I applied for this. It's not like..."

"It doesn't matter how you came to have the position. You have it and I'm paying you a lot of money, so I'm going to need you to do some work. And I'm going to need you to actually shower in the morning and put on some clean and fresh clothes. You are a representative of my company and..."

"Oh, I know you are not talking to me like that right now," I say. "You, who called me last night and..."

"Don't think you can speak to me this way in the office, Ella. In the office, I am your boss." He stands up and grabs the large stack of files and hands them to me. "I need you to do some actual work instead of making excuses about why you're so unprofessional and lazy."

"I'm not lazy. You are so rude. You..."

"I'll show you to your desk. What I need you to do is go through all these files and figure out..."

"You already told me you want me to figure out property taxes or something."

"I have a new plan for you," he says. "These are the latest planned communities that have been built all over the state of Florida. I want you to investigate which ones of them sold out the fastest and then tell me what community features they had."

"What?" I say, staring at him.

"Yeah. You're going to have to do some actual research, and then I also want you to figure out the community names and start coming up with some community names for the communities that I'm going to be developing."

"Okay," I say, standing up. I wonder if he's going to ask me anything else about last night. I wonder if he's going to flirt with me.

He walks over to me, looks me in the eyes, and then sniffs the side of my neck.

"What are you doing?"

"I'm smelling you," he says. "What do you think I'm doing?"

"Why are you smelling me? That's so creepy."

"Because I want to see if you smell like sex," he says, stepping back as if he hasn't just insulted me in the worst way possible.

"What?" My eyes widen.

"I want to know if you fucked your boss this morning." He chuckles slightly. "And no, I don't mean me."

"You are despicable, you know that, right, Colton?" I can hear the indignant tone in my voice and I don't care. He needs to be taken down a peg or three.

"No. I just want to know if you're giving it up to every man you work for or..."

My hand reaches up and I think about slapping him, but then I step back before my fingers touch his skin. I know he wants me to react. I can tell it from the way that he's looking at me. He's enjoying this encounter far too much.

"You know what? You're not even worth it. You're a jackass."

"You can slap me if you want," he says, smiling sweetly. "You might find that I quite enjoy it."

"You what?"

"What?" he says. "You've never had a little pain with your pleasure?"

He looks at his watch again. "We do have ten minutes if you really want to suck my cock."

"The only thing I'll be sucking," I say, "is a lollipop after I bite your cock off."

I glare at him and he chuckles.

"Now, now, Ella, we don't want your parents to think you suck as an employee."

"Why would they think that?" I say, glaring at him.

"If I fired you again on your first day."

I press my lips together and hold the files to me.

"Please show me to my desk."

"Yes, ma'am," he says. "Oh, and by the way..."

"Yes?" I say.

"Welcome to my business. Glad to have you here."

I don't respond to him because I'm not going to lie and say that I'm glad to be there. He shows me to a desk in a small room along the corridor and I'm glad to see that I don't have to share it with anyone. He points to a notepad on the desk and tells me that those are the passwords for me to log on.

"So if you have any questions, feel free to come through to the office. I'll be here until this afternoon," he says.

"Okay," I respond, not saying anything else. As soon as he walks out of the room and closes the door, I grab my phone and call Isabel. I am absolutely furious and I know that I'm not going to be able to do any work unless I let it out.

"Hey, how's it going?" she says, her voice happy.

"I am so pissed off right now it's not even funny."

"Oh no, don't tell me you banged Colton again."

"No, I did not. He is never going to be able to say he's been with me again because it's never going to happen. I cannot stand that man."

"Oh boy," Isabel says. "That bad?"

"Worse," I say. "If it wasn't for my parents and the fact that they now know about this job, I would've been out of here already."

"I am sorry, Ella, but maybe it will get better."

"I very much doubt it. What are you doing for lunch?"

"I don't know. I think Sarah and I had plans. Do you want to join us?"

"I think I'm going to have to because I don't care if it's during lunch hours, but I need a margarita or three."

Isabel giggles. "I totally know what you mean. So, have you thought about the Sugar Baby website idea?"

"I don't know," I mumble. Internally, I know that the idea is not good. Any type of deception isn't great and whenever I try to partake in it, it always seems to backfire on me. Yet, I haven't already dismissed the idea because I am stupid. Or a bit of a sadist. Or perhaps, both of those things.

"I'm telling you, girl, leave the profile open on your laptop when you're done for the day."

"I don't have a laptop. It's a desktop." As if that matters.

"Oh my gosh, Ella, laptop, desktop, it doesn't matter. Create the profile and leave it open. If Colton is nosy, which I'm almost certain he's going to be, he'll go in and he'll see what you were looking at. Imagine what he's going to think if he sees that."

"He's going to think I'm a slut." Which he is slightly entitled to think. I mean, I was dirty dancing with him without having any clue who he was. However, the reality of my life is that I'm far from a slut. I'm not even that good at flirting, which is something I've been meaning to work on for years.

"So?" she says. "Do you care? He's already acting like a jackass, right?"

"That's true," I say, laughing. I love it when Isabel is rude about Colton. She has not drunk his Kool-Aid. I know I should stick up for him a little bit, but I don't want to. He has enough people stroking his ego as it is. "Anyway, I'd better go. I don't want to get in trouble on my first day."

I hang up the phone quickly, look at the ginormous stack of files on the table and sigh. I grab a pen and the notepad and open the first file so I can start doing some work. This isn't the job that I've dreamed of, but it is a job, after all.

I notice that a lot of the community names in Florida have a beach, lake, or ranch after them. I start drawing some doodles that I think would be cool to go along with those names. I find that I'm not exactly hating doing the research. It's interesting to me to see how much money people spend on buildings in Florida. I wish I could buy a house for three hundred thousand dollars in New York City. I couldn't even get a shoebox for that price.

I wonder what it would be like to own my own home. To decorate it. To buy nice furniture. To have a yard. I'd have to keep this job for far longer than a couple of months if I ever wanted to get a mortgage. I find myself drawing different house exteriors, trying to imagine what my ideal home would look like. I giggle as the designs become larger and far more extravagant. I even add two dogs outside the front door of the last drawing.

"Yeah, right." I shake my head as I imagine living in a huge home. That is never going to happen unless I marry rich. But I didn't know any rich men, aside from Colton, and I certainly am never going to marry him.

Before I know it, the time has caught up to me and I jump up so I can meet my friends for lunch. I'm hungry and excited to think about something other than my new boss.

15

"Girl, what is going on with you and your sex god boss?" Sarah asks me as I nibble on my Waldorf salad. I'm hungry, but I don't seem to have an appetite to really enjoy my food.

"I don't even understand what is going on," I say, shaking my head. "Colton is an enigma." I realize that I wish I understood him better. I want to be in his head. I also wonder if he thinks about and talks about me as much as I talk about him. Somehow, I doubt it. He didn't get to be a billionaire by spending lunches with his friends talking about the last girl he banged.

"I'm sure he loves it when you say that," Isabel giggles, and I just shake my head.

"Look, I'm not going to lie. The sex was pretty good," I say and glare at them. "If either one of you laugh, I will go off."

"Why would we laugh?" Sarah says. "In fact, I'm kind of jealous. I want amazing sex."

"Me too," Isabel says, "especially with someone as hot as Colton Hart."

"He's not that hot. Trust me," I say. "And by the way, I

left the website open." I stare at them and shake my head. "I don't know if it was a good idea, but I figure if he does come to my desk and look, then he can get a surprise."

"I cannot believe you signed up for Sugar Babies," Sarah says, laughing. "That is absolutely crazy."

"Hey, it wasn't my idea. It was Isabel's."

"Yeah, because I think it's super funny. If he does see that, he's going to be beside himself," Isabel says, shaking her head. "So, how long is this going to last anyway?"

"I don't know," I say, staring at them both, "because frankly, I don't really understand what's going on." I sit back, chew on the lettuce and look around the restaurant. We're in a nice part of the city, a part that I wouldn't normally eat out in because everything's so expensive, but now that I have a job making so much money, I've told them both I'm treating them. "What if he fires me as soon as I get back?" I say. "What if this is all one big joke to him?"

"He won't," Isabel says quickly. "He's not that much of a jackass."

"I don't know. If you would've seen him earlier today."

"He likes you," Sarah says. "He was all upset that you were still wearing your clothes from yesterday. He totally thought you banged Danny, which, by the way, what is going on with him?"

"I don't know what's going on with Danny. I think that he's most probably super stressed out because he's a single father and, you know." I shrug.

"Are you sure he's not looking for something else?" Isabel says and I glare at her.

"No, he's not. He's Frannie's dad. That's it."

"Hey, no need to shoot the messenger."

"It's just annoying. You and Colton have said something to me about him, and he's not like that. He's just a nice guy, and I am just the babysitter of his daughter, and he appreciates that."

"Sure," Isabel says, "if that's what you think."

"It is what I think, and it is what I know as well," I say. I let out a deep sigh. "I'm sorry, guys. I don't mean to be all bitchy. I'm just super stressed out. I just don't know what's going on here."

"Did he try to kiss you when you got to the office this morning?" Sarah asks, and I shake my head.

"He didn't try to kiss me. He didn't try to do anything."

"Is that why you're upset?" Sarah asks.

"Of course not," I snap. "Why would I be upset at that?"

"I don't know. Maybe you thought this was something serious and he'd give you a kiss."

"No way." I roll my eyes. "This is not anything serious. We hooked up only because I was drunk that night. If I would've known it was him when I started dancing with him, I never would've danced with him in the first place," I say, huffing. "Anyway," I look at my watch, "I got to get back."

"You haven't even finished eating yet," Isabel says, and I shake my head.

"Look, here's my credit card. Give it to me later." I get up before either one of them can say anything and head out of the restaurant. I'm feeling annoyed, and I don't know if I'm annoyed at them, myself, or at Colton.

It's not that I like Colton or I want anything from him, but I am slightly put off by the way he'd spoken to me and treated me in the office. He'd looked handsome and while I didn't want to kiss him, I thought he would have at least attempted to get a kiss, and him asking me to give him a blow job wasn't the same thing. I was starting to feel like I had just been a plaything for him and that made me feel slightly annoyed. Not that I thought we had anything more than that. I didn't want anything more than that. He was Colton Hart, my archnemesis, and even though he was best friends with my brother, and even though one time I thought he was a good guy, that had all faded when he'd fired me.

I sigh as I make my way back to the office. I am surprised he hasn't even checked in on me, but I am not going to think about that. I make my way past the receptionist, who is glaring at me, and head to the elevator. I get out on the tenth floor and walk toward my office.

"There you are." Colton's voice stops me in my tracks, and I turn around.

"Yes?" I say, glancing at him. He has half a sandwich in his hand, and I wonder if he has been working here during his lunch. "I just went out to get something to eat with the girls," I say quickly. "I'm going through the files as quickly as possible."

"I am sure you are," he says, nodding. He looks me up and down. "I went into the office to look for you earlier."

"Yeah, I was at lunch," I say. "Is there something I can help you with? I don't have all the information yet. I'm not that fast."

"I know," he says. "I was bringing you an iPad." He stares at me for a couple of seconds and nods. "Let's go to the office and chat."

"Okay," I say, my heart racing. I can feel him staring at me as we make our way to the office. He closes the door behind me, and my stomach flips. This is it, I think to myself. He's going to kiss me. He's going to hike my skirt up and...

"So I noticed you were doodling on your notepad," he says as if it was nothing, and I blink. Most people never notice the fact that I love to draw little images of everything on my mind to pass the time.

"What?"

"You were doodling, drawing something."

"Oh yeah," I say. "As I was reading through the files, I noticed that a lot of the communities had similar names, so I was just doodling little logos that made me think of the names." This is it. I think to myself. He's going to tell me I'm wasting his time and his company's time, and he's going to fire me. I hold my breath, waiting for the inevitable.

"They're cool," he says emphatically, nodding toward the pad. "I didn't realize you were such a good artist." My heart soars at the compliment. Any time anyone mentions my artwork, I feel a strong sense of pride.

"Oh," I say in surprise. "Thanks. I am not really an artist, but I like to draw every now and then."

"You're good," he continues, and I love him for the fact that he appreciates my art. "In fact, why don't you do some graphics on the iPad? I've put Procreate on there for you, or I should say the IT department did."

"Procreate," I say, my eyes widening. "The graphic design program?"

"Yeah," he smiles, a genuine and warm expression on his face. He's being professional, and I can tell that he's not doing this as a joke or to get into my pants. "Who knows? Maybe you'll get an idea for a logo for one of our communities."

"But you want me to?"

"You can do more than one thing at a time, right?" he asks, raising an eyebrow.

I nod slowly. "Yeah."

"Oh, I also have something for you," he says. I stare at him in surprise.

"Not balloons?" I tease him, and he shakes his head.

"No, I'm going to save the balloons for a special time," he says, laughing.

"What do you have for me, then?" I pause. "And if you tell me your big dick, I am going to scream."

"Would I say that?" he says, laughing.

I'm about to answer him when my phone starts ringing. I glance at it and see that it's my mom. I'm about to put it back into my pocket when Colton nods. "You should take that."

"It's okay. It's during work hours."

"Hey, when your mom calls, you answer. You don't know how long she'll be around."

"Yeah, I guess," I say, answering the phone. "Hey, Mom. I'm at work, so I can't really talk."

"Ella, is everything okay?" she says, sounding nervous, and I frown.

"Yeah, I am okay. Why?"

"Are you dating anyone right now?" she says.

"What do you mean am I dating someone?" I glance at Colton. Had he told Sam? "No, Mom, I am... Hold on one second," I say as Colton hands me something. I press mute and look at him. "What's this?"

"This is your gift," he says, grinning. "Now get back to work when you get off the phone with your mom."

"Okay, thanks, I guess."

"Oh, you're welcome," he says, grinning. "You're very, very welcome."

I watch as he leaves my office and then I take my mom off mute again. "Hey, Mom. What is going on? Why are you calling me? I am really busy right now. You know that this is my..." I pause. I don't know if I should say this is my first official day or not. I can't remember exactly what I've told her about this position. I don't want her asking too many questions if she catches me in a lie.

"Darling, I just want you to know that even though Daddy and I are not rich, and even though we don't get much from Social Security, you do not have to date older gentlemen or—"

"What?" I almost shout into the phone. "What are you talking about, Mom?"

"I'm just saying that you don't have to put yourself in an

Anna Nicole situation. I know there are certain older men that look like Sean Coltony, but most of them—"

"Mom, I've got to go. I'll speak to you later." I hang up quickly. I'm seething. Is my mom referring to the Sugar Baby website? And if so, how would she know?

I glance at the present that Colton has given me and I open it quickly. It's a box of chocolates and a card. I stare at the box. It looks expensive. They're Belgian chocolates. I lick my lips excitedly. I absolutely love Belgian chocolates. I open the card and on the front I see a duck in a pond. Weird, I think to myself. I open it to see if he's written anything inside and all it says is, "Got you," with a smiley face.

I'm not really sure what that means, but I have an idea. I am pissed. He's obviously seen the Sugar Baby website, but he called my parents? I was not expecting him to do something like that. Or maybe he called Sam, and Sam called my parents because Sam was the sort of brother who, if he felt uncomfortable, would go to them before he would come to me.

I let out a deep sigh. I was so annoyed, and yet, I was a little bit excited because if Colton had been the one to spread the news, that means he had come to my computer and he had been looking around the office to see what I was up to. Some people might think that it's spying, but I like to think that it's because he doesn't quite know what I am doing or why I'm doing it. I'm an enigma to him just as much as he's an enigma to me.

I don't know what it means and I don't know what I want it to mean, but all I know is that I have Colton Hart where I want him, or maybe he has me where he wants me. I just don't know anymore, and I need to stop thinking about it because I don't want to think about his lips all over my body anymore.

16

"Why is it that cocktails always make me feel so much better about my life," I say as I hold my glass up and clink with Sarah and Isabel. We're all drinking at an exclusive club on the Lower East Side, and I'm three drinks in and feeling so much better about my life.

"Because alcohol makes the world go round?" Sarah says, giggling as she takes a long gulp of her lemon drop. She leans back and closes her eyes. I stare at her for a couple of seconds and then take a sip of my own drink.

"So, work's still sucking for you?" I ask her as she opens her eyes. I want to make sure that I ask Isabel and Sarah about what's going on in their lives before I start complaining about my own. Colton has added three hundred more files to my desk and didn't even speak to me in person.

"I'm a little bit peeved at the fact that he hasn't wanted to actually talk to me since my first day, and I just don't know why my job sucks," Sarah says. "My boss doesn't know I exist. I feel like a cog in a wheel and I don't matter. That sums it up," she says. I lean forward, grab her hand and squeeze it. I want her to know that even if she is not appreciated at work, she is appreciated by me.

"I'm sorry."

"It's not your fault," she says.

"Why would it matter that I am doing my absolute most to help a company that doesn't even know I work for them?"

"Well, they do know you work for them," Isabel says. "They're paying you a paycheck, right?"

"Barely," Sarah says, and we all start giggling.

"I know how you feel. I haven't even seen Colton since that first day," I say, wanting to choke myself but having brought him up already.

"What, you guys haven't banged already in his office?" Isabel says, her eyes glittering and I glare at her. "What? Don't tell me it's never crossed your mind," she says accusingly, and I blush.

"Okay, fine. I will admit it to you two because you're my girls. Yes, I did think that perhaps we would have a hate fuck in his office, but we didn't."

"But you wanted to," Isabel says, and I just glare at her again.

"Okay. It's true. The thought has crossed my mind several times, and when I go to bed at night, I think about how hot it could be, how I'd be bent over his desk and I'd push all of the folders onto the ground and I wouldn't have to be the one picking them up either, and then he'd lift my skirt up and pull my panties down and take me hard and fast, and I'd look over my shoulder and glare at him and tell him he was a pig and he'd fuck me even faster. It was slightly weird to me that that turned me on, but it did. It hadn't happened though, so my fantasies were not coming true."

"Okay, guys, do not do anything right now," Isabel says, leaning forward, whispering.

"What," I say loudly. "I can't even hear you."

"Ella," she whispers, glaring at me. "Keep your voice down."

"Why," I say, whispering, leaning forward. "What's going on? Don't tell me Brad Pitt's here and he wants me."

"You wish," Sarah says. "If Brad Pitt is here, I am taking him."

"Hey, I want him too," Isabel says. "We'll fight for him."

"I'm not fighting for Brad Pitt," I say, giggling.

"Why? Because you know you'll lose," Isabel says, as if this were a matter of grave importance. I shake my head because this conversation is ridiculous. If a fly on the wall were listening, he would tell us that none of us even stood a chance.

"Anyway," she says, "Stop distracting me thinking of things that will never happen." As if I were the one prolonging the conversation.

"Fine by me."

"What's going on with the empty glasses?" Sarah says, holding up her glass and looking dismayed. "I need another drink. Does anyone else need another drink?"

"I do," I say, drinking the last of my lemon drop. It's sweet and sour, and I need another one immediately. "Next round on you?"

"Yep," she says, pulling out her credit card and tapping it against the table. "Do we want some pretzels with beer cheese as well?"

"Guys, Colton is here." Isabel interrupts us, and my eyes widen as my heart pounds. Why is Colton always around? I wonder if he's stalking me and immediately dismiss the thought. Colton Hart doesn't need to stalk anyone.

"What?" I feel my body stiffen. "I haven't seen him in a while and I don't know that I want to see him right now." Which is only partially the truth.

"He's with someone," Isabel says, and she looks at them admiringly. "A really hot someone."

"What?" I say, feeling annoyed. I look around quickly, even though I know I shouldn't.

"You have no chill," Isabel whispers, but I don't care. I look into the corner and I see Colton sitting in a booth with a beautiful blonde. She looks stunning, and I can feel my heart dropping. I wonder if she's the same girl he had a date with the other night when he asked me to get the condoms. Jealousy tears through me. I don't know why I care. I don't care. I remind myself he can go on as many dates with as many beautiful women as he wants. It doesn't matter to me.

"Who do you think she is?" Isabel asks and I shake my head.

"I don't know. Don't care. Are you going to get the drinks, Sarah?"

"Sure," she says. "Are you upset?"

"No, I'm not upset," I snap and then sit back. "I just don't understand how a man can sleep with me and do other things with me and just ignore me."

"That's most men in the world," Sarah says. "Have you never met them before? I think she means, seeing as he's her brother's best friend."

"Yeah. He's my brother's best friend and he's now my boss."

"But he hasn't slept with you since he became your boss, right?" Sarah says. "So he's not being inappropriate." I glare at her.

"That's not the point. I just think that he's a pig and he shouldn't be able to go around New York City sleeping with random different women at different bars and dancing with them, and, and..." I stop. "Oh my gosh. I sound like a jealous shrew, don't I?"

"You do sound a little bit jealous," Isabel says. "I kind of think you might have..."

"Don't even say it." I glare at her. She looks over at Sarah.

"You have feelings for him?"

"Sarah!"

"What? You said to Isabel she can't say anything. You didn't say to me I can't say anything."

"It's not even a thing," I say, knowing I am not making sense. I feel myself standing up and they both glare at me.

"What are you doing, Ella?"

"I'm doing something that Colton deserves," I say as I head toward him. I'm not thinking straight. I know I'm not thinking straight because I've had three lemon drops and I haven't had a drink in a while. Well, maybe a couple of days, but I'd only had one glass of wine, so that didn't really count. I head over to Colton's booth and stop, my hands on my hips. "Hello. Fancy seeing you here, Colton Hart," I say. Colton looks up at me in surprise. He nods slightly.

"Hello? Didn't know you were here tonight, Ella."

"Of course you didn't," I say as my eyes travel to the blonde, she's even more stunning in person. "Who are you," I ask, groaning inside.

Shut up, Ella.

"Hi. I am..." She reaches her hand out, but I turn toward Colton again, ignoring her.

"I cannot believe you would do this to me, Colton." I fake tears. He looks shocked. Even I'm shocked at the way this is going. What has come over me?

"What's going on?" He blinks in confusion and I can tell that he has no idea what's about to happen next. Neither do I really, as I'm just making it up as I go.

"I'm pregnant with your baby and you're here in a club with someone else," I say. His jaw drops and I look over at the girl and her eyes are wide as saucers. I feel a little thrill inside as I rub my stomach. "And I was going to go and get a sonogram tomorrow," I say, looking at him. "And I thought you would want to know if it was a boy or a girl."

"Ella," he says, shaking his head, "Do not..."

"Do not what? Expose you for the fraud that you are, Colton? I want everyone to know." My voice raises and I feel satisfied for two seconds before the regret and panic start taking over.

17

"Melissa Sunshine," Colton says, standing up, "I would like you to meet my assistant, Ella Wynter." He turns to me. "Ella, this is my business associate, Melissa Sunshine. She works at the bank." My eyes widen as I realize the mistake that I've made. "Melissa, Ella is a little bit of a prankster. She likes to think of every day as April Fools." He stares at me. "I'm not going to tell you again, Ella, but these jokes and this stalking are not really funny anymore."

"What?" My jaw drops. What is he talking about? Stalking? Does he really think I'm stalking him? Is he crazy?

"I can only assume that you looked in my calendar to see where I would be this evening," he says, placing his hand on my lower back. I look up at him and I can see his eyes glittering as he looks down on me. "You must stop following me around. I know you have a crush on me, but..."

"I do not have a crush on you," I say, shaking my head. "I cannot believe—" I gasp as I feel his hand moving down to my ass and squeezing. "Colton!" I say.

"Look, Ella. I didn't want to embarrass you in front of

other people, but I did see that you were on that Sugar Baby website the other day."

"What?!" I look over at Melissa, who's looking down at the table. I can tell she feels embarrassed, but not for herself, for me. She's believing everything that Colton is saying, and I just want to shrivel up and die. "I don't know what you're talking about. I—"

"I saw your profile and I did speak to Sam," he says, "Because I'm worried about you. I'm concerned that you are going down a deep, dark road yet again."

"What are you talking about?!" I say, staring at him. "You—"

"I... What?" He says, squeezing my ass again, and I know I must be sick or something because I am loving the feel of his hands on me.

"Colton, you are crazy."

"Did you or did you not sign up for the Sugar Baby website? Before you say you didn't, you should know that I took some photos of your profile."

My jaw drops. "That's why my mom was acting crazy?"

"That's why I gave you that card that said, 'Got you,'" he says, winking, his voice low so that Melissa can't hear.

"You are a pig," I whisper back at him.

"Excuse me, Melissa," he says, "I just need to speak to my assistant for a moment."

"Oh, go ahead," she says as she looks over at me. "Honey, I'm going to give you a piece of advice. If you're trying to get ahead in the corporate world, you really ought not be a stalker. It's so unprofessional. I know Colton is a professional. He's a consummate professional, but in most other places, you would've been fired."

"Fired?!" I say, glancing at her. "Excuse me, but you have no idea who you're talking to or what is going on here, and I think that you—"

"Ella, that is enough," Colton says, "Excuse me, please,

Melissa." He pushes me toward the side of the bar and stares down at me. "What is going on?"

"What do you mean what is going on? I—"

"Why would you come up to me and my colleague, pretending that you are pregnant?" He pauses for a moment and his whole body stiffens. "You're not pregnant, are you?"

I stare at him for a couple of seconds and roll my eyes. "No, I'm not pregnant, idiot."

"How was I supposed to know if you were or not? Why else would you have said something like that?"

"We used protection, and it's not like we've been fucking nonstop."

"Oh, is that what this is about?" He says, tilting his head to the side and smiling at me.

"What?" I say, glaring at him.

"Are you upset because we haven't hooked up recently?"

"No!" I say, looking around, "Why would I care? It's not like I want to."

"You miss my cock," he says, whispering in my ear. I feel his hands smoothing down the side of my body, and I shiver slightly.

"You wish."

"No," he says, chuckling. "You miss me." He presses his lips against mine for a couple of seconds and moves back. "You want me?" He says, "You can admit it."

"You're out of your mind. No, I don't want you."

"You would love for me to take you into the bathroom right now and fuck your brains out."

"Oh yeah, because that's how I want to lose my brains..."

He chuckles slightly. "I'll tell you something, Ella," he says, pressing his lips against mine again. I feel his hand move up to my breast and I shiver slightly as he squeezes it. I moan as he moves his hand down toward my stomach and I wonder if he's going to slip it inside my skirt. I know I should push him away, but my body is hot, and I do want him. "What do you say?" He says, "I can take you outside to the alleyway, as well. Is that more romantic?" I hear the chuckle in his voice and something snaps inside of me. I push him away slightly.

"Are you out of your mind? Do you think I want to fuck you in a bathroom or an alleyway? What sort of woman do you think I am? How do you think Sam would feel if he knew that his best friend was talking to his sister like that?"

"I think Sam is already worried about you, seeing as he knows you're on a Sugar Baby website, and—"

"I cannot believe that you—"

"You can't believe that I told your brother?" He says, looking at me innocently, "You're the one that was using company time to look for a sugar daddy. What, so you didn't have to work? So you could have a man taking care of you?"

"You are crazy. You know that? You are absolutely crazy."

"I don't think that I'm crazy. I just think that you're desperate. I mean, I guess you just don't want to be single again this Christmas."

"What do you mean single again?"

"I mean, it's not like you have a man right now, right?"

"Oh my gosh, I cannot believe you just said that to me. Who do you think you are?"

"I think I'm the man that fucked you most recently, and I think that you loved it, and I think that you want it again, and you know what, Ella?"

"What?" I say through gritted teeth.

"I want you too," he says, "So, we can play games. Or—"

"You know what? I'm over you, and I'm over this entire situation."

"Just answer me one thing," he says.

"What?!" I snap.

"Why did you come over?"

"Because, as you said, you were fucking me very recently,

and I just don't think it's cool that you're on another date with someone else."

"What do you mean, 'another date'?" He says, chuckling. "I don't remember you and I ever going on a date." I bite down on my lower lip. He's correct, of course. We've never been on a date.

"What are you trying to say, that I'm easy?" I say, with eyes wide.

"I wouldn't say that," he says, shaking his head. "I mean, yeah, we were at a masked party, and yeah, we were dirty dancing, and yeah, I touched you, and you didn't even know who I was. But hey, we were having fun, right?" I just listen to his words and don't respond because the way he's saying them makes me feel like I'm a little bit of a slut.

"Hey, if men can have fun, so can women," I say.

"Hey, I agree and let's be real. You knew who I was before you fucked me."

"Yes, I did, and I should have walked away as soon as I found out," I say, "Because you've just been a headache in my life."

"Really?" He says, his arms moving around my waist as he brings me in toward him. "I've just been a headache in your life?"

"Yes," I say, glaring up at him.

"I mean, I could say the same thing, Ella."

"Yeah, but you're not going to because—"

"You want to know why I'm not going to?" he says, leaning down to kiss me on the nose.

"Why?" I say.

"Because you look mighty pretty when you're angry, and if you didn't know, I'm hard as hell right now." He presses himself against my stomach and I gasp as I feel his hardness. I reached down involuntarily and squeeze. "Oh, fuck," he says, shaking his head. "You shouldn't have done that."

"Why not?" I say innocently.

"Come," he says, grabbing my hand and moving me toward the corridor.

"Where are we going?"

"I think you know where we're going, Ella," he says. I glance at him for a couple of seconds and shake my head, but then, because I listen to my body more than I listen to my brains I go with him. We slip into one of the restrooms and he locks the door. "We don't have much time," he says.

"We're not going to," I say quickly.

"You don't want to do that," he goes to open the door again and I just glare at him. I push him back against the door and I lean up on my tippy-toes and kiss him.

"I'm not playing games," I say. He growls as he reaches down and lifts my skirt up. I can feel his fingers pulling my panties down and I moan slightly. I reach down and unzip his pants and pull his cock out. He groans as my hand moves back and forth quickly.

"Fuck, you are so hot, you know that?"

"Shut up," I say, "I don't want to hear your voice."

"Ooh, I like it," he says, laughing as he pushes me back slightly, picks me up, and places me on the sink.

"What?"

"Easier access," he says, laughing as he slips my panties off completely and puts them into his pocket. I feel his fingers between my legs, and I moan slightly as his thumb rubs against my clit roughly. He pulls me forward, his eyes laughing at me. "If you just wanted a fuck, you could have said that. You know that, right?"

"Shut up, Colton," I say as he reaches into his back pocket and I watch him pull out a condom wrapper. I look at it in surprise and he chuckles.

"Well, you got me balloons. I had to get some real ones just in case."

"For who?" I say, mumbling, wishing I hadn't asked but

he just shakes his head. I watch as he rips open the condom wrapper and slips it on.

"Fuck," he says, "Why do you do this to me, Ella?"

"Because you want me so badly," I say, leaning my head back. He growls as he grabs my hips and pulls me forward. I feel the tip of him at my entrance and he slams into me. I groan slightly as I feel him all the way inside of me. I shouldn't be enjoying this so much, but I really am.

"Oh, fuck yes. You're so tight," he says. "You're so wet. You've wanted this all night, haven't you?"

"You mean you've wanted me?" I say as I grab on to the sink.

"Open your eyes, Ella," he says. I open them slowly and he stares at me as he continues to fuck me hard and fast.

"You know..." I breathe out. "That looking at me with your eyes open as you fuck me means you're a psychopath," I say before I start screaming. I'm coming hard and fast and he reaches down and his thumb rubs my clit and I know I cannot control myself any longer.

"Fuck!" he says as his body stills and I feel him trembling as he comes. He pauses slightly and then pulls out of me and I watch him pull the full condom off him. "Fuck, that was hot," he says. He lifts me off the sink and places me back down on the ground.

"You're such a pig," I say, glaring at him, my entire body shaking.

"Oh yeah?" he says, "I guess that's a compliment." He grins and then he leans down and grabs my head and kisses me hard and fast. His lips crash against mine for what feels like an eternity. I hold on to him so that I don't fall, enjoying the feel of him against me, and then he steps back. "I have to get back," he says, "Melissa's going to be wondering what went on. I'm going to have to tell her that I almost fired you."

"What?" I say.

"Well, I have to have an explanation for why I've been gone so long," he says, chuckling. "I can't go back and tell her I just fucked you in the bathroom."

"Really, Colton?"

"What," he says, grinning. "Hey, Merry Christmas to you. I guess this was an early Christmas present."

"What?" I say, my eyes wide as he chuckles.

"Hey, I know, all you want for Christmas is a little bit of Colton Hart."

"You wish," I say, shaking my head. "Trust me, dude. All I want for Christmas is not you." I say as I push past him and leave the bathroom. I cannot believe that I just fucked Colton Hart again. I am literally crazy.

18

"Oh my gosh, Isabel. I'm so annoyed with myself," I say to my friend on the phone as I sit back on my couch. "I cannot believe I let that happen."

"I know," Isabel says softly. "We've been talking about it for a week. You need to forgive yourself," she says, and I wonder if she's been listening to some sort of self-help podcast recently or something.

"Girl, I haven't seen him in over a week. It's just embarrassing."

"Girl. No one told you to sleep with him in the bathroom at that bar."

"I had had three lemon drops," I say, "and I don't think I really ate much dinner."

"Girl, you have to stop blaming the alcohol for the bad decisions you're making."

"I'm not blaming the alcohol. Look, I fully admit that I was super turned on and I wanted him. I never realized that hate sex could be so good."

"Hate sex?" she scoffs while laughing her head off. "Now you hate him?" She raises an eyebrow as if to say we both know you do not hate him.

"You know I dislike him very strongly."

"I mean, I get it," she says. "Trust me. I get it, but there's a thin line between love and hate, you know."

"Oh my gosh. Ever since you watched that movie, that's all you can say."

"What? That was a classic '90s movie. It isn't exactly something that I see on the must-watch movies of the millennium," I say.

And she giggles. "You're such a hater. You know that, Ella?"

"I'm not a hater. I'm just annoyed with myself. Why can I not say no to this man?"

"Because he gives it to you good."

And I groan. "I don't even want to think about it. How embarrassing. Like what did he say when he went back to that Melissa?"

"I'm guessing he didn't just say, 'I banged my assistant in the bathroom.'"

"Well, duh," I say, groaning. I sigh. "And why hasn't he been in the office? Why is he ignoring me?"

"Girl, I don't know."

"And did I tell you what he said?"

"Yes. You told me everything that he said."

"He said that was his Christmas present to me. Like I'm some sort of loser, that I need him to give me sex as a Christmas present."

"I know," she says, "You've told me this a billion times already."

"You know what I said to him?"

"Yes, I do," she says, interrupting me. "You said all you want for Christmas is not him or something like that."

"Because it's true. How egotistical does that man have to be to think that I would want him as a Christmas present? Like, do you think you are everything in the world to someone like me?"

"He most probably does," she says, laughing. "I mean, I'm not going to lie. You went over there, interrupted his business meeting, and I'm still not even sure about that."

"Right," I say, agreeing with her. "Who takes a colleague to a bar?"

"Exactly," she says. "Anyway, you interrupt his business meeting, go on about how you're pregnant, and then you go into the bathroom with him and you proceed to let him sleep with you. And it wasn't like some sort of lovemaking. It was definitely what most people would classify as a hot fuck."

I groan. "You're not making me feel better, Isabel."

"What? I'm your best friend. I will always be honest."

"Thanks," I say.

"What? I wouldn't mind having a hot fuck in the bathroom with some hot dude. Trust me, if it was Colton, you wouldn't want Matt."

"That's true. But I think some part of you is getting off on this."

"I am not. I mean, yes, I did get off, so to speak. But that's only because he has the most marvelous, thick, long, and delicious dick I've ever felt or seen in my life."

Isabel groans. "Really? I thought you didn't like the man."

"I don't like the man, but that doesn't mean I'm going to lie about his appendage." I giggle. I don't know why thinking about Colton and his magical body parts makes me giddy, but it sure does. "Okay, so I have an idea. You know what I'm going to do?"

"No. What are you going to do," she asks me softly.

"I'm going to..." I pause for dramatic effect.

"Please tell me you're not going back on that Sugar Baby website," she says as if it wasn't her idea in the first place. "I fully admit it wasn't my best-ever recommendation." She adds on before I can call her out.

"Isabel, none of your recommendations are great. You know that, right?"

"What? I was trying to help. It's just you don't think it through after I bring up my great ideas."

"Well, you obviously didn't think it through either." I protest. "But it's true," I say, "I'm as much a fool as you are for not analyzing everything that could go wrong before I go ahead."

"Well, hopefully Sarah is not as much of a fool as the both of us." She cuts in, and I am surprised to hear Sarah's name.

"Why?" I ask her curiously.

"Because I gave her a recommendation recently as well." She admits with a small giggle.

"You what?" I say, confused. "What are you talking about? What recommendation?"

"Oh, I'll tell you later when we meet up with her. Okay?"

"Sure," I say, "Anyway, I'm going to join a dating app. Like, for real. Real."

"What do you mean for real? Real? You're always joining them. That's nothing new."

"But I'm going to swipe on almost everyone. I don't care if they're rich or hot or anything. I just need to meet someone so that I can date someone so I can have him drop by the office and be like, 'Hey, is my girl Ella there?' And then I'll make sure that he goes to Colton's office by mistake. So Colton thinks that I have a man and he will know that I don't want him for Christmas. I don't need him for Christmas. In fact, I don't ever want to see him again."

"Well, he's your boss, so you're going to see him again."

"You know what I mean," I say, "I don't want to see his *O* face again."

"Oh my gosh," she says, laughing. "That is so weird."

"What is so weird?"

"That you've seen your boss's *O* face? Really? What?"

She says, laughing. "I mean, you've seen your boss's *O* face because he *O*'d with you. How many people can say that?"

"I don't think many people want to be able to say that. Plus, when I saw his *O* face the first time, he wasn't my boss."

"True," she says. "I couldn't imagine banging my boss. Ew."

"Okay, Isabel, you're not helping."

"What?" I'm just saying, "Could you imagine if I banged my boss?"

"No. I don't want to imagine you banging your boss. I don't want to imagine you with your boss at all."

"Okay? I'm just saying."

"You're just saying a lot of things. But I'm going to swipe now because I need to find me a man."

"You will find you several men. I have no worries about that, Ella."

"What does that mean?" I say, frowning.

"I mean that you're super cute. You're super fun. You're super friendly, and almost every man in the city would love to date you. I mean, they might not want to sleep with you because you do seem to go a little crazy once that happens." She pauses too soon, way too soon.

"And not funny." I groan as I hear my phone beeping. "Oh my gosh. Colton is calling me."

"What? Why? I thought you hadn't heard from him in ages."

"I haven't heard from him in ages, and I don't want to hear from him. I don't want him to tell me to go and get him any rubbers or anything like that."

"Girl, answer the phone and see what he wants."

I don't. "Fine." And I say, "Hold on." I click over. "Yes. Can I help you?"

"Hey, sexy." He says in his deep, gravelly voice, and I feel my entire body shaking.

Why is he so hot? And why do I always respond? "What do you want?"

"I need you to..."

"Nope. Do you know what time it is?"

"It's eight p.m."

"Exactly. I'm not on the clock."

"I need you to..."

"Nope. You can call me during office hours, or you can stop by my office. I'm not doing anything for you right now, Colton Hart."

"You don't even know what I..."

"I don't care what you're about to say. It doesn't matter," I say quickly. "As far as I'm concerned, if it's not work related, it doesn't matter."

"It is work related and..."

"And then, you speak to me during work hours, nine to five."

"You're employed for eight to five."

"Whatever," I say and let out a deep sigh. "I don't care what you have to say. You can tell me tomorrow. But I don't care." I click over.

"Hey," I say to Isabel as I click back. "What did he want? Does he totally want to come over and bang you right now?"

"I don't know what he wants and I don't care. I told him if it's not office hours, I don't want to know."

"But what did he want?"

"I just told you. I don't know. It's eight o'clock at night."

"Oh my gosh. Really?"

"Really, what?" I say. "He just thinks he can call me and have me whenever he wants."

"So you do think he wanted a late-night, shebang-bang girl?"

"I don't know what a shebang bang is, and I don't care. He's not having me again."

"Uh-huh," she says, "I'll believe it when I see it."

"Well, hopefully you never see it because that would be disgusting." I laugh.

"Ella, sometimes I do think you are one of the silliest, goofiest people I know."

"Yeah. And?"

"And I just love you for it," she says.

"You go ahead and swipe and tell me about it later. Okay."

"Okay," I say.

"Also, Isabel."

"Yes?"

"Thank you for listening to me and putting up with me. I know I've been going on about him a lot recently. I'm just so infuriated."

"It's okay," she says. "Trust me. We all get crazy when it comes to hot guys."

"Uh-huh," I say and hang up. I lean back on the couch and stare at my phone. I've downloaded three different dating apps and am ready to start swiping. I do wonder what Colton was calling about. I do wonder if he'd wanted to meet up. I'm glad that I hung up the phone though, because I know me. I know that even though he gets on my last nerve and I can't stand him, I'm still super attracted to him and I still want him.

There's just something about the way that he talks and the way that he commands himself that I can't resist. If I'm honest, I've always found him to be a little bit handsome. Okay. Really, really handsome.

I know that I'm one of the biggest fools alive by having a crush on my brother's best friend, especially when I can't stand him. But I can't help myself. And if I'm honest, I'm also enjoying the job. It's something that I've never even thought about doing, but it's something that I'm really good at.

I look down at the iPad, open the Procreate app and stare

at the different designs I've come up with for logos for the different communities. I'm impressed with them, even though I designed them. I've always been slightly artistic, but I'd never created a logo before.

I need to email them to Colton tomorrow, but I'm nervous about what his feedback is going to be. For some reason, I don't want him to hate them. I don't want him to tell me that I've wasted his time and his money. I don't want him to say that he thinks that it's not working out and that I should find another job. Because I've tried really hard and I'm proud of what I've done. And well, it's been a long time since I've been able to say that.

I sigh as I open one of the dating apps and start swiping. "Everything will be fine," I mutter to myself. I just need to find a hottie, and that way, Colton won't think that I care about being with him anymore. Even though he is the starring man of my fantasy every night.

I think a part of the reason why I am trying to forget him is because it seems that he isn't interested in me whatsoever. He hasn't even spoken to me since we hooked up in the bathroom. Not a word, and that makes me feel kind of used and I hate that feeling. I really, really hate that feeling. I am not going to allow this man to get into my head. I am not going to allow him to make me feel bad about myself. I am not going to allow him to make me question who I am and what we have because I want him to want me. I want him to want me as more than just a fuck buddy. I want him to want to take me on a date. I want him to be jealous. Like I was jealous when I saw him in the bar. Like I was jealous just thinking about what he was doing. "Stop it. Ella." I mumble to myself. "Just stop it. I have to get out of this mindset. I don't want to think about him anymore."

19

There is a bagel and coffee on my desk when I get to work the next morning and I look around in surprise. This is the first time anyone's ever left me anything, and I'm not sure why it's here. I open the bag to look at the bagel, debating taking a bite, when I hear a knock on the door. I look up and there is Colton, his blue eyes shining as he stares at me.

"Morning, Ella," he says, giving me a wide smile. "How are you today?"

"I'm fine," I say suspiciously as he walks inside and closes the door. "I'm not looking for a morning quickie though, just in case you were thinking that was on the table."

He bursts out laughing and shakes his head. "Do you think that all I want from you is sex?"

"I don't know." I shrug. "It seems to me that every single time that you're around me, you are either hinting about having sex with me or someone else, of course or ..."

"Or what?" he says. Rolling his eyes. "I am a CEO, there's more on my mind than fucking you, Ella Wynter."

"I'm glad to hear that because I'm sure my brother

would not like to know that you have fucked me several times in some really crass places."

"Shall we call him now and ask what he thinks?" he says, pulling out his phone.

I stare at him for a couple of seconds. "You're not going to call him," I say. I watch as he presses a button and puts it on speakerphone. My jaw drops as it rings once and then Sam answers the phone.

"Hey, what's up, Colton? What are you doing?"

"I'm just here at work with Ella and I wanted to tell you that ..."

"Hi Sam," I say quickly. "How's it going? How's law firm life?"

"I'm okay. Have too much coffee this morning, sis?" he says. "What's going on, Colton? Please tell me you're not firing her again. Please tell me that."

"Of course he's not firing me. Thanks, Sam."

"What?" He starts chuckling. "I mean, you've made it a couple of weeks already, so that's something to be proud of."

"Very funny." I glare at Colton. I cannot believe he's called my brother.

"Hey sis, we do need to speak though. Colton did tell me about the Sugar Baby website ad."

"It was just a joke." I sigh. "I have no idea why Colton would send that to you because he knows it's a joke."

"Yeah, I mean, I wasn't sure because I know when I saw you the other evening at that bar, you said ..."

"Really, Colton?"

"Hey guys," Sam interrupts us. "I actually have a mediation today. Can I call you back later?"

"Sounds good," I say, smirking at Colton.

"I'll speak to you later, Sam," he says. "Maybe we can go for drinks tonight."

"Perfect," Sam says and hangs up.

I stare at Colton and shake my head. "What was that about?"

"What was what about?" He shrugs innocently. "I mean, Sam is my best friend and you're his sister and I feel like I should come clean. I mean, that's what you would want, right?"

I stare at him for a couple of seconds. "So you want to tell him that you met his little sister at his office party and you took her back to your place and you fucked her? And then the next morning, you allowed her to pretend she was your new assistant so that you could fuck her again?" I smile at him sweetly. His eyes narrow and he chuckles.

"No, but I can tell him that his little sister came up to me at his work party and I had no idea who she was because she had on a mask and she started dirty dancing on me and rubbing her booty up on my cock, getting me all hard. And hey, she didn't even know who I was."

I glare at him. "You're such a jackass."

"But you say you didn't know who I was. Right?" He asked innocently.

"I didn't know that it was you."

"So I could have been any old man that you were rubbing your ass up on."

I say, "Look, I just was having fun and it ended up being you."

"And you knew it was me when you came back to my place." He shrugs. "So let's not pretend that you're Little Miss Innocent here. We're both complicit in the fact that we have fucked each other's brains out and we'll likely fuck each other's brains out again."

"I don't think so," I say. "I actually have someone."

"You have someone?" he says, raising an eyebrow. "Okay, sure."

"Yeah, I do. So there."

"Okay then," he says, nodding. "Good for you. Anyway,

the reason I came to your office this morning wasn't about your personal life or who you're fucking. Though I guess you always want to bring it up."

"No, I don't." I stare at the bagel and the coffee. "Did you put this on my table?"

"I did. I wanted you to have breakfast for our meeting this morning."

"What meeting this morning?"

"I wanted to see the designs you've come up with for the new community in Florida. You did say you were working on a logo in your last email to me."

"Yeah. I have been working on stuff," I say, suddenly feeling nervous. Now that we're talking about work, the mood has changed.

"So, will you show me or ..."

"Fine," I say, grabbing the iPad from my bag and opening it. I open the Procreate app and pull up the designs. Colton grabs the iPad from me and stares at them. I watch as he swipes and looks through the different designs. He's silent for a few minutes and I have no idea what he's thinking. Maybe he hates them. Maybe they're not as good as I thought they were.

"So this is what you've been working on?" he says in a deadpan voice.

I look into his eyes and they're serious now. I nod slowly. He hands me back the iPad and takes a seat.

"You can sit, Ella."

This is it, I think to myself. He's going to fire me. He thinks they suck. He thinks I suck. I've pushed my luck too far. I feel a sudden weight on my shoulders as I go and take a seat. I stare at him and brush my hair out of my face, feeling nervous. I look at his lips, not because I want to kiss them, though I do want to kiss them, but because I'm scared to look into his eyes. I'm scared to see the disappointment.

"I want to say that—" He pauses. "You can look at me,

Ella." His voice is gruff now and I look into his eyes. He leans forward and taps his fingers against the desk. "You've done a good job," he says, nodding slowly. "I'm impressed."

"You are?" I say, disbelief in my voice as I stare at him. "Like, with my logo designs?"

"Yeah," he says, a small smile curling up on his face. "They're really good. There are two of them I'd like you to develop a little bit more, but I think one of them could be a winner." He nods. "You are talented. I'm thinking that perhaps ..."

"Yeah?" I ask him. Is he going to give me a compliment, like a real compliment?

"I'm thinking that perhaps we should have you change departments."

"Oh?" I say.

"Yeah, I think you'd be good in our marketing department in the graphics section," he says.

I stare at him in shock. "Really? You want to promote me?"

"Well, it wouldn't actually be a promotion," he says. "As my assistant, that's one of the highest jobs you can get at the company."

"Yeah. Okay." I say, laughing.

"What? You don't think so?" He's teasing me now. "You don't like being under me."

I stare at him for a couple of seconds. "Actually, I prefer being over you." I wink at him and he chuckles. The mood is much lighter now and I'm giddy and happy at his compliment. "I'd love to go into the marketing department though, in graphics. I'd love to work on these logos. In fact, I had a couple more ideas and I was thinking that you could actually have each house represent a different section. Like, we could make it like a community and have different ..." I pause as he starts chuckling. "What? What's so funny?"

"You're really enjoying this, aren't you?"

"Yeah. Why would you ask me that?"

"Because we both know you didn't start this job because you had any interest in it, but I think you are really enjoying the work."

"I am. I mean, if I'm honest, I never thought I would enjoy it either, but it's been cool. It's been fun and it's been interesting doing the research and seeing what people are attracted to. And I thought we could do some market research when we go to Florida this Christmas and see which logos people liked and what community names."

"That sounds like a really good idea," he says, nodding. My phone starts beeping then and he pauses. "Do you need to take that?"

I look at the screen and see that it's a message from one of the guys on the dating app and I shake my head. "No, it's okay."

"Is it your brother asking why we called?"

"No, it's just a guy I'm talking to."

His eyes narrow then and his arms cross. He leans back. "A guy you're talking to?" There's no humor in his voice right now. "Yeah, you know, like, for dating and stuff."

He presses his lips together. "Who, Danny?"

"Like I told you before, Danny is a guy I work for sometimes, for babysitting. We don't date."

"But now there's another guy that you're dating?"

I shrug. I don't want to give him too much information. I don't want to tell him that I haven't even met the guy and that I'm just chatting with several people to make him feel like an idiot when I have a boyfriend at Christmas and don't actually want him. I mean, there's no way I'm going to tell him that.

"So, do they know about me?"

"Do they know what about you, Colton?" I roll my eyes. "There's nothing to know. Like you said the other day, we've never even been on a date."

"Okay," he says. He stands up then and I feel slightly disappointed that he doesn't want to continue the conversation. "Continue working on the designs," he says as he walks to the door.

"Okay." I look at him.

He opens the door. "Let's go to dinner tonight."

I stare at him in surprise. "What?"

"I said, let's go to dinner tonight."

"I can't," I say, "I'm busy."

"Really, with what?"

"I have a date, possibly." Which is true. A couple of guys have asked if I want to go for a drink and I haven't yet messaged them.

"With Danny?"

"No, not Danny." I'm annoyed now. "I already told you I'm dating someone else."

"Hmm," he says. "Really?"

"I just said that to you." He closes the door and then walks over to me. I frown slightly. "What are you doing?"

He shakes his head as he walks around the side of the table and he grabs my hand and pulls me up. "You have a dinner date tonight with someone?"

"Like I said, yes, I do. You don't have to know everything about my private life. Like you said, we're not dating and we are not ..." I can't even finish the sentence because his lips are on mine and he's kissing me. I melt against him. I don't know why he has this power over me, but I absolutely cannot resist this man. My fingers reach into his hair and he growls as he pulls me against him tighter. I feel his hands running down my back, reaching for my ass and squeezing. He kisses down the side of my neck and I feel him undoing the buttons of my blouse. He slips his fingers up into the blouse and pulls it off and onto the ground. I stare at him in surprise, but I don't say anything. He reaches behind, undoes my bra and pulls it off. I'm standing there topless in front of him. "What is going on?" I say, blinking.

"What do you think is going on?" he says as he reaches down and takes my right nipple into his mouth and sucks. I reach up and undo his shirt so that I can touch his chest and moan slightly as he slips his finger down between my legs and rubs. "Like that, do you?" he says, as his fingers play with my other breast. I moan slightly. He pulls back slightly and wipes all the files off the desk onto the floor, and I look up at him with wide, beguiling eyes. I can't believe that he's doing what I have been fantasizing about doing in his office. He grabs me and pulls me up onto the table.

"We can't fuck here," I say, mumbling. Even though that's what I want.

"Oh, we're not going to fuck," he says as he pulls my skirt up. I stare at him in surprise. He chuckles slightly as he grabs my panties and pulls them down my legs. He spreads my legs wide and before I know what's happening, his mouth is on my clit and he's sucking.

"Fuck," I say as his tongue slides back and forth in my wetness. He starts grabbing on to my legs and spreading them wider and I don't know what to do, so I close my eyes, grab his hair and pull on his silky tresses as he eats me out on my desk. I can feel his tongue sliding inside of me and he's fucking me hard and fast. It's crazy that his tongue feels as good as some guys' cocks. I can feel myself building up to an orgasm and I think he knows it because his tongue moves faster and faster as he starts sucking on my clit at the same time. "Oh fuck," I say as I'm moaning. I feel myself coming hard and fast and he's licking and licking so that not one ounce of my orgasm will reach anything but his mouth. He finally pulls away and looks down at me, a wide smile on his face. I watch as he buttons up his shirt and he winks.

"Remember me on your date tonight," he says. I stare at him as he exits and I feel myself going red. I cannot believe that I've just allowed this man to go down on me. He walks to the door and smirks.

"I cannot believe you just did that, Colton," I say, shaking my head.

"Why?" he says.

"Because."

"Because what?"

"Because you can't."

"I can't what?"

"You can't just go down on me in the office."

"I want you to think about me tonight."

"That's just ridiculous," I say.

"Then tell that guy no. Tell him you're meeting me for dinner instead." He pauses. "And I'll give you round two."

"You're only asking me to dinner because I have a date."

"You don't know that," he says. "Maybe I'm asking you for another reason."

"Well, I'm not canceling," I say. "You have a good day." I get off the desk and feel slightly awkward, but I'm not going to allow myself to feel embarrassed.

20

"Hi. You must be..." I pause as I try to remember his name. The guy stands there just staring at me, with a weird look on his face, and I'm not sure if he thinks that I am flirting with him or if he realizes that this is an awkward moment because I can't remember his name.

"Zevo," he says finally. "I'm Zevo. And you must be Emma."

"Ella," I say. "Nice to meet you, Zevo."

"Hey, when I saw you wanted to meet up, I was like, 'Hell yeah, that hottie with the thotty body.'"

I stare at him for a couple of seconds. What was that he had just said? "So, yeah, I thought it would be better to meet sooner rather than later."

"I agree because we don't want to waste no *T* on thee, can't you see?"

I stare at him, blinking for a couple of seconds. What is going on? Why is he talking like that? "So, have you been here before?" I ask as we step into the restaurant.

"No, I ain't, but we got to eat, so I thought, why not?

Hey, does that rhyme? I don't know, but is it a crime?" He looks at me, and I can feel myself starting to sweat. I try to remember what he had told me about himself. He was a teacher that taught English. Why was he talking like this?

"So, you are a teacher?" I ask him, hoping that I was remembering correctly.

"Yeah. I teach elementary school kids, but my real dream is to be a rapper. You know?"

"Oh, cool," I say. "That's interesting. You didn't mention that." Not that we talked for very long. I had just thought he looked really cute in his photos, and he had thought I'd look cute. And when I said I wouldn't mind meeting tonight, he had jumped on it.

An image of Colton's face pops into my mind at that moment. If he could see me right now with this guy, he'd be laughing, but I am not going to think about him. I am not going to think about how he told me to remember him eating me out on my date. I groan as I realize that that is exactly what I am thinking about.

"Hey, you okay? You just made a weird sound," Zevo says, and I nod slowly.

"Yeah, I just was thinking to myself that I haven't met many English teachers who are rappers on the side."

"Yo, yo, yo. What's up with that, right?" he says. And I stare at him.

"Oh my gosh," I think to myself. What the hell is going on? "So, where are you from originally?" I ask him.

"Yo, I'm from Detroit. What up? Call out to all my homies in Detroit. Eminem, can you hear me? 50 Cent."

I blink. "Oh, you know Eminem?"

"No." He laughs. "But wouldn't that be cool if I did?"

"Oh, yeah. Supercool. Eminem is like so cool," I say, not knowing what else to say.

"He the man. Not like Kid Rock, yo. Kid Rock a solo. What? Am I right?"

I wonder if I can run out of the restaurant and go home. I don't know if I'm going to be able to spend the evening with this man. This is a disaster. I think to myself that it's almost what I deserve. I don't really deserve it, but maybe this is punishment for letting Colton have his wicked way with me so many times. Not that I've been complaining.

"So, my parents are from Sicily, initially. Well, not really," he says, laughing.

"They're from Sicily, or they're not?" I ask as we have a seat.

"Well, my great grandma, who I call Nona, I mean, hold on. Wait. She's my grandma, not my great grandma. My Nona, she's from Sicily."

"Cool," I say, nodding, not caring. "So, I realized that I meant to meet my best friend in an hour, so I might not be able to get an actual full meal but an appetizer."

"Yo, I was hoping you'd say that, man. I don't make that much money. You hear me? Yo. Just because you're honey."

"It's okay. I can pay for my own appetizer."

"But I like to be a pimp, P-I-M-P. I don't know what you can take that from me. Yo, hold up. That didn't really make sense, did it?"

I just stare at him. I don't want to tell him that almost nothing he has said has made sense.

"So, you are a bod-y," he says, looking me up and down, "with a capital *B*."

"Thank you," I say, not knowing if that's a compliment.

"Yo, so I know that on Tinder, a lot of girls want to hook up right away, and I normally say, 'Yo, I'm not down with that. Zevo ain't no ho,' but baby, if you want to take me to your crib tonight, just let me know, 'cause I can pow, pow, pow, pow, pow. You hear what I'm saying?"

I press my lips together. This is not going well. I hear my phone beeping, and I pull it out of my handbag and look at the screen. It's a message from Colton. I'm about to close it, but I open it instead. My jaw drops as I see what appears to be his penis.

Colton: Like it?

Me: That is disgusting. How could you?

Colton: You want to eat it?

My jaw drops. I cannot believe him. I'm about to go off when he sends another photo. And I realize that the first photo was not of his cock, but a hot dog. I start giggling.

Me: You are really stupid. You know that, right?

He sends back a smiley face.

Colton: I can tell your date's going well.

And I put my phone back in my handbag. He's right, obviously. Obviously, my date is not going well if I'm texting him. I look back up at Zevo. He's staring at me, a wide grin on his face.

"Yo, you want to hear this rap I wrote last night for you?"

"Not really," I say honestly. He looks slightly sad. And I take a deep breath, "But I have a feeling you're going to tell me anyway."

"Yeah. So, listen to this. Emma. Emma. You are thick like a themma, themma. No, I did not say femma, femma, because you don't have a beema, beema."

I hear my phone beeping as he's rapping, and I grab it. I don't even care if Colton thinks I'm having a shitty date because I am having a shitty date, and I cannot believe I'm here with Zevo, the idiot.

Colton: So, I was hoping we could talk about the designs for the recreation area for the new community. I think you really have talent.

I stare at the message, and I feel myself growing warm. As much as I can't stand Colton, and as much as he gets on my nerves, I really am appreciative of the way that he's nurturing my talent. And if I'm honest with myself, Isabel was right.

There's a really fine line between love and hate, and as much as I dislike him, I really do look forward to his messages as well.

Me: Sounds good. I'm really grateful for this opportunity.

Colton: I'm glad. I'm really glad.

He then sends a photo of himself without a shirt, and I shake my head.

Colton: Think of me naked on your date. Oh wait, I'm sure you already are, obviously, if you're texting me and not paying attention to him. I guess you're wishing you took me up on my dinner offer now.

I stare at his texts, and while every single word is true, I don't want him to know that. I decide not to respond. But then he sends one last message.

Colton: If you want to come over to my place tonight, let me know. I'll leave the door open for you, and then I'll give you the fucking of your life. Oh wait, I've already done that.

My jaw drops, and I blush as I stare at his message, and then put my phone back into my handbag.

"So, what'd you think?" Zevo says, finishing. I don't know if he's realized that I was texting on my phone or not, but I don't care.

"I think that you have a very unique talent," I say, staring at him. "And I think that I'm actually a lot hungrier than I thought I was, so let's order."

"Great," he says, "I knew you would be down with this white chocolate."

I cannot believe that he's called himself white chocolate. I cannot believe that this is real life. I want to start laughing. I want to call Isabel and Sarah and tell them what a hot mess this evening was. But I know I need to be polite. I know that there are so many things going on that I just need to eat, drink, and be merry, and get my mind off all of them for even a little bit, because I think I'm starting to fall for Colton, and that scares me, because all we have going is a game. And one thing I know is that you don't fall for someone that's part of a game because you're only looking to get hurt.

21

"I can't talk long, Isabel," I whisper into the phone. "He's just gone to the restroom. I just don't know what to do."

"I mean, you don't have many options." She giggles. "He does sound like a little bit of an idiot."

"Girl, he's more than a little bit of an idiot. He's a royal idiot. He has been rapping the entire night, and when I say rapping, I'm using that term generously because he cannot rap to save his life." I giggle slightly. "Why do I always meet these weirdos?"

"Because most of the guys out there are weirdos," she says. "Why don't you just leave?"

"Because I want to be able to look Colton in the face tomorrow and say, 'The date lasted for hours' and mean it."

"Oh my gosh. Really?"

"Yes, because he's been texting me all night saying, 'Are you thinking about me? Oh, I know you're thinking about me. Oh, I know you want me.'"

"But you have been thinking about him."

"Okay, sure I have, but I don't want him to know that."

"Okay, then, so what are you going to do? You want to come over here, and we can..."

"No, I can't tell Colton that I left my date and went to hang out with you."

"Okay, so what do you want to tell Colton?"

"I want to tell him that my date came back to my place."

"Girl, you're not actually thinking about hooking up with that guy just so you can tell Colton that you hooked up with him."

"Of course not, goofy, but maybe if I invite him over to karaoke or to play a game or something."

"Oh my gosh. Really, Ella?"

"I know it sounds crazy, but Colton is just driving me crazy, and well, I need to get him off my mind."

"You're falling for him, aren't you?"

"Yes. No. I don't know. It's weird. He's so supportive in the workspace, and I love that because it's really encouraging, but he's just so full of himself."

"Girl, just go over to Colton's place tonight and let him bang you senseless."

"Isabel, you're not helping, and no, I'm not going to do that."

"Fine. Then take that weirdo wannabe rapper over to your house and play board games with him."

"I mean, when you put it like that, it does sound stupid, but... Oh gosh," I whisper. "He's coming back." I hang up, put the phone into my handbag and smile up at Zevo.

"Yo. Yo. Yo. Did you miss me? I bet you did because I am tasty."

I stare at him for a couple of seconds. "Well, I was just thinking maybe we could play a board game later." Even as the words come out of my mouth, I regret them.

"Oh my gosh, that would be amazing," he says. "I love board games. What game? Monopoly?"

"Yeah, we can play Monopoly. I think I have it."

"Yo, if you don't have it, we can go back to my place. My roommate might be home, and he might want to join us, but..."

"No, it's fine. I'm pretty sure I have it." I say quickly. There was no way I was going back to his place.

"So you want to get some dessert here, or do you want to get it to go?" he says. "Hey, that could be a rhyme." He thinks for a second. "Yo, yo, yo. You want to get dessert here, or you want to get it to go? Do you want me to eat all up in your face? You like chocolate, or is that a disgrace?"

I stare at him for a couple of seconds, and then I start clapping because I don't know what else to do. It's not like I can tell him to shut up and that his rapping sucks, though I know that I'm never going to see him again after tonight.

"Why don't you get something to go?" I say quickly. "And we can have it at my place when we play Monopoly." I'm already regretting the suggestion, but there's nothing else I can do.

"Sounds good. I'll get some chocolate cake, and then we can feed each other." He licks his lips. "Hey, you'll have white chocolate and dark chocolate. How'd you like that?"

"Oh, I don't know how I've gone my life without having white chocolate and dark chocolate," I say sarcastically, and he laughs.

"I mean, if you had a devil's threesome, maybe."

"Excuse me?" I say, blinking at him.

"You know, one woman, two guys. If you had a black guy and a white guy, then you'd have milk chocolate or dark chocolate and white chocolate together. Yo, if you had a foursome, you could have white chocolate, milk chocolate, and dark chocolate. Did I just come up with something? Shit," he says. "Man, I could be famous. What would I call it? The chocolate night of adventures?" He pauses and tilts his head to the side. "Does that sound cool?"

"No," I say, not even caring. "It doesn't sound cool. It

sounds absolutely..." I bite down on my lower lip as I hear my phone beeping. I look at the screen. It's Colton again.

Colton: So you coming over or what?
Me: Nope, sorry. We're going back to my place.

I don't know why I told him that. I guess I just felt like I needed him to know that the date was going fantastically, even though the date was going horrendously. I didn't like how he felt like I was just going to fall into his arms whenever he wanted me, and I didn't like that I wanted to fall into his arms. I didn't like that I was falling for him because I knew there was never going to be anything between Colton and I, ever. Not really, aside from these silly little games we were playing.

"I'm going to just go and wash my hands," I say. "You can order the cake, and hopefully, we can just go when this is done."

"Sounds good, chica. I wouldn't want to be ya, but I'd like to see ya. If you want to eat ya, I can grant you a little tasty wasty of my..."

I stand up and leave the table. There's just no way I can listen to any more of this. As I make my way to the bathroom, I pull my phone out. "Isabel, I'm an idiot."

"Oh boy. What did you do?" she says.

"I invited him over to my place to play Monopoly."

"Okay. And?"

"And all he's been doing is rapping ever since, and I think he might think that something's going to go down, but it's totally not going to go down."

"Girl, of course he thinks something's going to go down. You invited him to your house after a first date. He totally thinks he's going to get some."

"Well, he's not getting any."

"I know he's not getting any because the only one you want to give something to is Colton."

"I don't want to give Colton anything."

"Oh my gosh. Why did I call you?"

"Because I'm your best friend and I'm the voice of reason."

"So how do I get him to not come over?"

"At this point, just go and play the Monopoly, girl. Maybe you'll have fun."

"Maybe." I sigh. "But if it sucks, I'm going to message you to come over, okay?"

"Okay," she says. "I promise I'll come over if you want me to."

"Thanks, girl."

"You're welcome. Should I ask Sarah if she wants to come as well? Maybe we can play a four-player game."

"Oh my gosh. He might like that too much," I say, groaning.

"What?"

"Oh, you don't want to know about the chocolate foursome."

"The chocolate foursome? What the hell is that?"

"I'll tell you later," I say, chuckling. "You will not believe the night that I've had." I stand in the bathroom and look at my reflection in the mirror. I don't know where I've gone wrong in life to find myself in this situation, but something has obviously gone drastically wrong.

Zevo and I walk toward my apartment, and I can see a familiar figure standing outside on the street, waiting. I groan as we approach.

"Hey there," Colton says as he looks at me and then he looks at Zevo. There's a surprised expression on his face. I think he thought I was lying.

"I've been waiting for you," he says,

"Like I told you, I was on a dinner date. This is Zevo."

"You are going back up to your place, or Zevo is about to leave?" Colton says.

"We're going up to my place."

"Yo, we're going to play some Monopoly. You want to play, man?" Zevo says, looking Colton up and down.

"Sure. Thanks." Colton grins, and I glare at him.

"I mean, you guys don't have to both come up and..."

"No, but sounds like a great time," Colton says, staring at me. "Thank you so much for thinking of me."

"No problems, man. I'm always down for an audience," Zevo looks at Colton, and Colton raises an eyebrow.

"An audience?" I stare at him. What the hell is he going on about?

"Not for public sex or anything," Zevo says, though the look on his face belies what he's saying. "Though, Ella." He looks me up and down as if I'm a delicious piece of cake and I try not to sniff in disgust. "I can't lie. You're so fly that if you want to hump me dry, I don't care if we're in front of a crowd because, yeah, I'm the sort of guy that can get down."

I stare at him, and I can see Colton's lips twitching. "Sorry, what did you just say?" Colton says to no one in particular. I can tell that he is finding the entire situation hilarious and all I can think is that he must think I'm desperate. What sort of woman brings an idiot like Zevo home?

"Oh, I'm a little bit of a rapper. Some people know me as the second Eminem."

"The second Eminem?" Colton says, and I can definitely hear mirth in his voice.

"Yo, you know, Slim Shady?"

"Oh, I've definitely heard of Slim Shady," Colton says. "I didn't realize that there were two."

"Well, I'm going to be like the better Slim Shady."

"Oh, cool," Colton says as we walk up the stairs toward my apartment. "Ella, you didn't tell me that your boyfriend was a rapper."

"He's not my boyfriend. This was just our first date."

"The first of many, if I'm lucky," Zevo says and looks

back at me. "Because, honey, I will take you out and not for any money."

Colton starts coughing, and I can tell he's trying not to laugh. This is my worst nightmare come true. We stop outside my door, and I fish in my handbag for my keys. I turn to look at them, and I yawn. "Oh, I am feeling a little bit tired. If you guys just..."

"Oh, you could make some coffee or something," Colton says. "I'm really looking forward to playing Monopoly with you guys, and I've been waiting so long for you to get back that..."

"Yeah, come on, Ella. Don't be a bee-yach just because you think we're going to beat you," Zevo says, and I press my lips together. We walk into the apartment, and I watch as Zevo looks around. "This is a cool place. I dig. I could live here, man. My roommate is getting on my nerves."

"If you'll hold on a second, please," I say as I rush into the kitchen. Colton follows behind me. There's a smirk on his face.

"Ooh, so that's the sort of guy you're going for now."

"What is that supposed to mean?"

"I mean, you tried with the rich older men and that didn't work. Now you're trying with the young losers."

"He's not a loser. He..."

"Oh, so sorry. I shouldn't say loser. I forgot that he's the second Eminem. After all, we all know the real Slim Shady is not a loser." He starts chuckling as if he's just told the funniest joke in the world. "I can't believe I just said that sentence."

"I can't believe you just said that and tried to rap," I say, my lips twitching, even though I want to be mad at him. I stare into his blue eyes for a couple of seconds, and all I want to do is kiss him.

Passionately.

And with tongue.

I want to wrap my arms around his neck and breathe him in.

Instead, I step back. "What are you doing here, by the way?"

"I wanted to make sure that you got home okay."

"Really? Why?"

"Because I know how men can be in the city, and when you said you were bringing some strange guy back..."

"I never said I was bringing a strange guy back."

"When you said you were bringing your date back, I wanted to make sure that he wasn't a psychopath or a serial killer."

"Why, do you think I have poor judgment or something?" I cock my head to the side and look him up and down. I hope he doesn't answer me because even I think I have poor judgment in that moment. The fact that my date with Zevo has lasted more than five minutes is proof of that.

"Do you think you have good judgment, Ella?" There's a knowing look on his face and I wish that I could tell him off for being so high and mighty. "Don't you wish you went to dinner with me instead?" he says, leaning forward and whispering in my ear. It feels sensual and intimate and I hate myself for enjoying the feel of his warm breath on my skin so much. It's like I crave any and all contact I have with him.

My brain is screaming that, yes, I wish that I'd gone to dinner with him. My heart is screaming, yes, I wish I'd gone to dinner with him as well, but I'm not going to let him know that. "I had a really good time with Zevo."

"Zevo?" he says. "Zevo is his real name?"

"I don't know," I say, attempting to avoid eye contact with him.

"Yo, you got Annie Corona, Ella, Ella, Ella, Ella, Ella." He says my name over and over again. He walks over to my TV. "Man, this is big. What is it? Like thirty-four inches?"

He looks at me and wags his tongue. "Or am I talking about my C-O-C-K? Ha, ha, ha. Don't you want to know?"

I stare at him for a couple of seconds. "And I thought I had a big cock," Colton says under his breath, and I just stare at him.

"No wonder you don't want to go out with me," he says. "I didn't realize I was competing with a man with a thirty-four-inch cock."

"Very funny, Colton. That is so ridiculous."

"Is it?" he says, slipping his arm around my waist.

"Yes," I say. "What are you doing?"

"What do you mean what am I doing?" His hand reaches down and squeezes my ass. He pushes me toward him, and he starts grinning. "I'm just saying hello."

"You cannot be squeezing my ass in front of..."

"In front of who? Your *date*?" He rolls his eyes as if he finds the word laughable.

"Colton."

"What?" he says, running his fingers across my lower lip. "I want to kiss you so badly right now."

"Not going to happen." I look down at his crotch for a split second and he laughs.

"What do you think your friend would say if you dropped down to your knees and started blowing me?"

"Colton, that is not going to happen. I..." I swallow hard as he grabs my hand and runs his finger across my palm. My heart skips a beat and I know that there will never be a moment when I don't find this man irresistible.

"Yo, where's your restroom? I need a piss," Zevo interrupts us, and I take a deep breath and walk away from Colton. My fingers miss his touch and I internally chastise myself.

"Just to the right. That door over there," I say, pointing down the small hallway. Zevo looks out of place in my home and I knew it had been extremely immature of me to invite him over.

"Cool, cool," he says. "I won't be long. Actually, I might be a little longer than I thought because I need to do a dump." He starts laughing. "Yo, I never thought I'd do a dump on the first date. You got any matches?"

"Matches?" I say, glancing at him.

"You know, for me to throw into the toilet after I do my dump, just in case it's stinky."

I shudder slightly and shake my head. "Um, no, but there's spray."

"Cool," he says. "I'll be back in a little bit." He winks and stops by the door. "Don't do anything I wouldn't do," he laughs.

I shudder again as he goes in. I rub my forehead. I just wish I was alone.

"So what do you think is something..." Colton says, and I blink.

"Sorry, what did you say?"

"I said, what do you think is something he wouldn't do?" He pulls me into his arms and kisses me. I feel his tongue in my mouth and I try to resist, but I can't stop from kissing him back.

"You cannot kiss me here. My date is in the bathroom."

"Your loser date is in the bathroom doing a dump in your toilet. Really? You're telling me this is the guy you want to be with?"

"I'm not saying I..." His hand reaches up my top and he starts playing with my breasts.

"You look superhot. I can't believe you dressed up this hot for some loser. I don't know what... Why don't you ever dress up this hot for me?"

"You think I'm going to wear something like this to the office?"

"Well, I guess not," he says, laughing as he slips his hand

down the front of my skirt between my legs. "Come on, baby. You think we got time for a quickie?"

"Colton," I say as his fingers slip past my panties and start rubbing me. "Oh my gosh. What are you doing?" I grip his arms and I can feel my body trembling. "You need to stop. You need to leave. You shouldn't even be here."

"I've been thinking about you all evening," he says. "Thinking about you on a date with some loser. I don't know why you turned me down."

"I didn't turn you down. You said you wanted to go to dinner and I told you I had plans."

"Dinner with me would've been much better than being with this guy."

"You don't know. Maybe I had an amazing time with this guy. Maybe..."

"You did not have an amazing time with a white rapper from Detroit, who's called Zevo, who calls himself the second Eminem. I know you, Ella. You forget that."

I let out a deep sigh. "Well, maybe I didn't have the best time, but that doesn't mean that you can... Oh my gosh." I start sighing as he inserts a finger inside of me. "Colton."

"Tell me you don't want this," he says as he kisses the side of my neck. "Tell me you don't want to come right now."

"Colton, I really don't think..."

He adds another finger, and his thumb starts rubbing my clit. I grab hold of his shoulders. My body is shaking. "Oh my gosh."

He pulls his fingers out, and I watch as he sucks them. "You taste good," he says.

"Oh my gosh, please," I say. My body is trembling.

"You want me to finish what I started?" he asks, grinning. I nod slightly and he growls as he pulls me over to the couch. We get down onto the couch and he pulls my skirt up. I know I'm messing with fire, but I don't even care. He slips my panties to the side and starts rubbing me again, slipping two fingers inside of me. "Oh my gosh," I moan as I lie there. "Fuck," I say as he increases his pressure against my clit. "Oh my God. Yes, yes."

"Come for me, baby," he says. I feel my body starting to orgasm at the same time that the bathroom door opens. My eyes fly open. "Stop," I say, even though he's moving his fingers faster and faster. My entire body is trembling.

"Yo, what's going on?" Zevo says as he walks into the living room. I can't believe it, but Colton's fingers are still inside of me and my legs are still spread. In five seconds, he's going to see Colton fingering me, and I just don't know how I will live out that embarrassment.

"Oh, shit," I moan as I feel myself coming fast. Colton grins and one second before Zevo walks into the living room, he's pulled his fingers out and pulled my skirt down. My entire body is trembling. Zevo looks at us, a grin on his face.

"So I did do a dump, but it's not as stinky as I thought, so I don't think I need those matches."

"Um, okay." I blink, unable to look at him. I know my face is red. I know if he looks at us closely enough, he's going to realize what's just happened.

"So you want to have that cake now?" he asks.

"Oh, I don't think she wants it," Colton says smoothly. "She's already had her dessert."

I glance over at him and he grins. I watch as he slips his two fingers into his mouth and sucks on them. "Mmm," he says. "Tasty."

I look over at Zevo, who looks slightly confused. "Yo, what's going on?" he says. "Why are you here again?" He takes a step over to us and looks Colton up and down. It's then that I realize that Colton's hand is on my thigh, and it's moving farther and farther up. His fingers are tracing a line along my leg. "What do you think I'm doing here?" he says, looking over at Zevo.

"I don't know, man, but I was trying to be cool by letting you come to play Monopoly with us. But I think you got to go. Me and Emma..."

"Her name is Ella."

"That's what I said. Me and Ella are about to..."

Colton jumps up and heads over to him. His gait is strong and confident, and I'm once again reminded as to why I cannot seem to quit this man. "Dude, you need to leave."

"What do you mean I need to leave? I..." I can tell Zevo thinks this is a joke at first, but then nervousness appears in his voice.

Colton stares at me and then stares at Zevo again. "Dude, I just fucking finger fucked your date. Okay? Do you really think she wants you?" I want to crawl under a pillow and hide at his words.

Zevo's jaw drops, as does mine. I cannot believe Colton has said that. My face is as red as a cherry tomato and I am mortified as Zevo looks at me.

"And I'm about to fuck her. So unless you want to watch, I think it's time for you to leave."

Zevo shakes his head, "Yo, man, what the fuck is going on? Was this just a game to you, Ella? Was I just a plaything because I'm a rapper and I'm going places, and you wanted to see if you could hitch yourself to my trailer? Hell no, bitch."

"What did you just say to me?" I gasp as I jump up.

"Did you just call my girl a bitch?" Colton says, angry now.

"Yo. Wait, what?" Zevo says, and I can tell he's slightly nervous as Colton looks as pissed as hell. I stare at him for a couple of seconds. Had he just called me his girl? But I wasn't his girl. I didn't even understand what was going on.

"You better leave right now before my fist connects with your nose and your mouth and you ain't rapping ever again,"

Colton says. "You hear me? Don't you ever call my girl a bitch."

"Yo, man. I don't know what the fucky, freaky thing is going on here, but I didn't know she was your girl. Why did she go on a date with me? Why..."

"Get out of here," Colton says as he leads Zevo to the door. "Now." Zevo blinks and then leaves. I'm standing there just staring at Colton. He turns to me and raises one single eyebrow. "What the hell is going on here, Ella? Who is that loser, and why are you wasting time with him?"

"You can't just come in here and send my date packing. You can't."

"You're going to seriously tell me that you were into that guy?"

"Okay, maybe not into him, but..."

"So then, why is he back at your place?"

"I mean, he just... I was just thinking that we..."

"You were doing it so you could screw with me. Well, you're not going to screw with me anymore, Ella. Are you into me or not?"

I stare at him for a couple of seconds. "What do you care?"

"What do I care?" he says. "Are you fucking kidding me right now? I'm hard as fucking hell, and you're asking me what do I care?"

"I'm not asking you if you're hard. Obviously, you like to bang me. That much, I know."

"Do you think this is about me wanting to fuck you? Seriously?"

22

"I just don't understand what's going on," I say as I glance at Colton.

"What do you not understand, Ella?" he says, shaking his head. He heads toward the couch and takes a seat. He pats the cushion next to him. "Come on."

"Why are you telling me to come on in my own house?" I say, glancing at him.

"Okay. Don't come on then," he says, leaning back and unbuttoning his shirt.

"Why are you taking your shirt off?"

"I'm not taking my shirt off," he says, shaking his head, his lips twitching. "I was just getting comfortable."

"Why are you getting comfortable?"

"Because I have a feeling we are going to have a conversation and I would like to be comfortable while we have the conversation."

"I don't think we need to have a conversation, Colton. I —"

"Oh, my giddy heart. Ella Wynter, will you sit your ass down and let's talk?" he says, shaking his head.

I press my lips together, head over to him like a petulant

child and sit down on the couch. "What do you want to say to me?"

"You have been in my brain for years."

"Okay. And what does that mean?" I say, though my heart is racing and I'm curious what he's talking about.

"It means that I have had a thing for you for ages."

"No, you haven't," I say, shaking my head.

"Yes, I have," he says, his eyes boring into mine.

"Well, then, why did you fire me on my first day? That was so embarrassing." I feel mortification at the memory. I'm still not over it.

"Because I had to," he says, shaking his head as if that was answer enough. I don't think he realizes just how badly he hurt me. Or how I'd had a huge crush on him at the time that had dissipated almost instantaneously.

"No, you didn't have to. My parents thought I was—"

"Ella, I fancied you. I wanted you. You were young and you were throwing yourself at—" His voice is sharp and soft at the same time and I'm not sure how it's possible for me to both love him and hate him so much in that moment. Colton Hart is twisting my brain and my heart upside down.

"I was not throwing myself at anyone."

"Do you remember when one of my business associates came in and you were kind of flirting with him?"

"Um. He was flirting with me. I wasn't flirting with him."

"Well, that made me jealous and it made me angry and I knew there was nothing I could say or could do. And I didn't want to put you in a position where you were going to have to flirt with jackasses like him."

I stare at him for a couple of seconds. "You fired me because you were jealous about my interaction with that dude?"

"Yes, and because I wanted you for myself. And I knew you were far too young for me to make a move."

"Okay. You wanted me?"

"You're gorgeous and you're funny. And I knew that you had just graduated and you needed to figure out the world. Plus, I didn't want Sam killing me."

"You liked me?"

"I don't know why," he says.

"You liked me?" I laughed giddily. "I can't believe you fired me still."

"Why? Because you were such a good, hard worker?" he says, winking.

"You didn't even give me a chance to see if I was going to be a good, hard worker."

"I know," he says. "And I apologize. I shouldn't have done that. I should have just assigned you to somewhere else in the company."

"Okay. Because I wasn't good enough to be your assistant?"

"No, because all I could think about was bending you over my desk and fucking you. Okay?" he says. "Just like all I'm thinking about right now is getting into your bed and making sweet, sweet love to you."

"You want to make sweet, sweet love to me, really?" I say, giggling slightly.

"Um. Well, maybe not sweet sweet, but pretty sweet," he says, chuckling.

I shake my head and run my finger down the side of his jawline. "You know what, Colton?" I say as I get onto his lap.

He shakes his head, but his hands go behind me and push me in closer to him. I spread my legs slightly so that I can feel his hardness between them. I rock myself back and forth on his lap.

"What are you doing, Ella?" he says as I start undoing the buttons on his shirt.

"Helping you to get comfortable," I say.

"Are you sure?" he says, staring at me, his fingers going

through my hair as he pulls it back so I can look him directly in the eyes.

"Am I sure that I want to be on top this time?" I say, winking at him.

"Yeah, I'm sure."

"Why? Because you want to dominate me?" he says, growling as I rip his shirt off.

I giggle slightly. "I don't know if there's any dominating you, Colton Hart."

"You never know," he says.

As he pulls my shirt off in one fell swoop, I see buttons going all over the place and I blink. "I love that shirt."

"I'll buy you another one," he says, shaking his head as his fingers undo my bra quickly. He grabs it and pulls it to the ground and I press my breasts against his chest. He moves me back slightly so that his fingers are playing with my nipples. "You are absolutely gorgeous," he says. "You were too young then and there was a bro code I had to abide by, but you're older now."

"So that makes it okay?"

"Maybe not," he says, pausing.

"What do you mean?"

"I mean, I can't say that you're older and wiser." He chuckles slightly, and I glare at him.

"You're such a jackass."

"I'm a jackass you love to fuck though."

"You're so crude."

"Am I?" he says. "Do you want me to leave then because I'm so crude?" He leans forward and takes one of my nipples in his mouth and starts sucking. I moan slightly as I gyrate my hips on his cock. I can feel him growing harder and harder. "Fuck. Why do I love being with you so much?" he says as he reaches down and unzips his pants.

I reach down and grab his cock and pull it out.

"Fuck. You are so hot," he says as he slides my panties to the side. "I just want to be inside of you."

"Oh yeah?" I say as I move up slightly and rub myself against him.

"Fuck. I want to be inside of you. You're not on the pill, are you?" he says as his fingers run down my back.

"No. Why?" I say as I press my lips against his, my fingers running up and down his manly chest.

"Because I fucking want to come in you so badly," he says. "I want you to feel all of me inside of you."

I shiver slightly at his dirty words. "You definitely don't want Sam hearing you say that," I say, laughing.

"You're right about that," he says. "Come on. Let's go to the bed."

"You got rubbers on you?"

"I got balloons," he says, winking.

And I groan. "Very funny."

"What? I think it's funny that you were so jealous that you got me balloons instead of condoms."

"I didn't get you balloons because I was jealous. I—"

"You can say whatever you want, sweet thing," he says. "Come on." We make our way to my bed. And I pull down my skirt and panties. He stares at me for a couple of seconds as he rips down his jeans. "Fuck. There is no one hotter than you, Ella Wynter."

"I don't know if that's true," I say, "but thank you for the compliment. They're very rare coming from you."

"And you know I don't lie," he says as he grabs my hand and pulls me onto the bed.

I reach over and grab his cock and move my thumb and finger up and down it.

"Fuck," he says, groaning. "Don't stop."

"What? Not even to ride you?" I say as I let go of his cock and move over. I position him between my legs and rub my clit back and forth on the tip of his cock.

"I could slam into you right now," he says. "One full thrust." His voice is barely a grunt.

"You would love that," I say, moaning slightly as he reaches up and plays with my breasts. My phone rings then and I moan as I go to reach for it.

"No," he says, shaking his head. "Not now."

"What?" I say.

"I said not now." He rolls me over onto my back. And before I know what he's doing, he's pulling a condom onto his cock and sliding deep and hard inside of me. "All you're going to think about right now is me, Ella Wynter," he says as he grabs my legs and pulls them over his shoulders. I can feel my back shaking as he thrusts deep and hard inside of me. My breasts are jiggling back and forth, but I don't even care. "Oh yeah. You like it when I fuck you like this, don't you?" he groans.

I can hear my phone still ringing, but I don't even care. I can't even think. I can barely remember my own name. He leans down and presses his lips against mine as he pulls my legs back and starts playing with my clit.

"Oh, fuck," I scream as he slams into me harder and harder. And then I feel myself coming hard and fast.

"Come for me, Ella. Come for me," he says. "Yeah. Just like that. Just like that." He groans and then he pulls out of me and I watch as he pulls the rubber off and then spurts all over my stomach. "Fuck yeah," he says as he stares down at his seed all over me. He leans down, kisses me and plays idly with my nipples. "So I guess you did have a good dinner date after all."

"You are a pig, you know that?"

"No. I don't think so," he says, chuckling. "I think I am the man of your dreams."

"You wish," I say.

"Do I though?" he says. And we both start laughing.

23

"Hey, I have an idea," Colton says to me as we lie there in my bed. He's playing with my belly button and I just stare at him.

"Yes? Are you going to tell me your idea?"

"No, I was hoping you would guess," he says as he runs his fingers down from my belly button toward my pussy.

"Colton, I'm tired," I say, laughing. "I am not ready to go again."

"We should shower though," he says as he smiles.

"Why?" I ask him.

"Because we're dirty," he says, rolling the *R*.

I just shake my head. "You're really ridiculous."

"I'm ridiculous? Hey," he says, "Yo, Ella, Ella, Ella. Shall I get my umbrella, ella, ella? Do you prefer if I was a white rapper, rapper, rapper to go on a date?"

I hold my hand up and I can't stop laughing. "Do not do that. That sounds absolutely ridiculous."

"I thought you liked it," he says, grinning. "You seemed to really like Zevo."

"Yeah, that's why I'm here in bed with you."

"Oh, so you admit it. You do like me more than you like him."

"Well, yeah, I like you more than I like him," I say, playing with his chest hair. "You are ridiculous. You know that, Colton?"

"I don't know about that," he says. "So, what are we going to tell Sam?"

"What do you mean what are we going to tell Sam?"

"About us," he says.

"We're not going to tell Sam anything. There is nothing he needs to know."

"Okay, so you don't want him to know that I'm seeing you?"

"Well, we're not exactly seeing each other because you haven't taken me on a date." I moan. My phone starts ringing again. "Oh my gosh. Who is that?" I say as I reach over and grab the phone. "Oh, it's Danny."

"It's midnight. Don't answer," Colton says, rolling his eyes.

"I have to. Oh my gosh, what if something happened to Frannie?" I answer the phone frantically. "Hey, Danny, is everything okay with Frannie? What's going on?"

"Hey, Ella, I was wondering if you were there."

"Yeah, I'm here. What's wrong?"

"I'm sorry, I just realized the time," he says. "I really need to speak to you. Can you come over?"

"What? Now?" I frown. "It's midnight."

"I know, I know. I know it's late, but it's really important."

"Can it not wait until tomorrow?"

"I just wanted to ask you something. It's really important."

"Oh, well, I'm kind of in bed."

"You don't have to get dressed up all fancy or anything."

"I mean, I wasn't going to get dressed up all fancy," I say, laughing slightly. "It's just really late."

"I mean, if you can't come now, it's fine," he says. "I just haven't seen you in a while."

"Oh, did you need me to babysit for Frannie? You know, I'm really busy now with my new job." I can see Colton staring at me and I'm trying to ignore him.

"It's fine. It's just, it was really important."

"Okay, I'll come over," I say reluctantly. I do not want to go anywhere, but if it's important, I want to be there for him. "Just give me twenty minutes."

"Thank you."

"I knew you would do it, Ella," he says. "I'll be waiting."

"Okay." I hang up the phone and I look over at Colton. He's glaring at me.

"Are you an idiot?"

"What are you talking about?"

"I mean, are you an idiot?"

"Something's obviously happened. He really needs to see me."

"At midnight?" Colton says, shaking his head. "Really?"

"He's stressed out. I told you his wife left him and he's a single dad."

"Oh my gosh, Ella. Sometimes, I think you wouldn't have any sense if it wasn't for a stupid sense."

"Excuse me, what does that mean?"

"Well, you sure don't have common sense," he says.

I jump out of the bed and just stare down at him. "You can go home, or you can stay or…"

"Oh, there's no way I'm letting you go by yourself. I'm going to call a car and we'll drive over there."

"No, you don't have to do that, you—"

"Yes, I do," he says, glaring at me. "Put on some clothes and let's go."

"You don't have to come, Colton, I can…"

"I am your brother's best friend. If anything happened to you, he would kill me."

"Why would he kill you? I'm not your responsibility."

"Because I'm here with you right now."

"Oh, so you're going to be like, 'Oh, hey, whatever happened to your sister was my fault because I just fucked her a couple of hours before that'?"

"Ella, don't you get it?" He sighed. "Anyway, we're not going to go into this right now. We can talk about it later."

"Talk about what later?" I say as I pull on my top.

"Are you not going to put on a bra?"

"It's fine. I'll just put a sweater over it. He won't be able to tell."

He stares at me and shakes his head. "Okay, if you think so."

"Anyways, he most probably just needs some advice about Frannie. She's probably done something and he's stressed out. Maybe she was crying about her mom and he just needs someone to tell him it's going to be okay."

"And you're the person to tell him that?"

"Maybe. I don't know."

"Oh my gosh. Fine," he says. "Come on, the car is waiting downstairs."

"Already? It hasn't even been..."

"You forget I'm a billionaire." He grins. "If I want a car, it's there right away."

"Okay," I say, glancing at him. "But how is that possible? It's been two minutes."

"My driver has been waiting for me all night," he says. "Who do you think brought me here in the first place?"

I remember then that he'd been waiting outside my building when I arrived. "Your driver was sitting in a car waiting for you the entire time, so he knows you spent the night, so he thinks I'm..."

"He doesn't think anything. I don't pay him to think. Plus what? I screwed my girl."

"Why do you keep calling me your girl? I'm not your girl."

"Yes, you are," he says. "Unless you don't want to be my girl."

I stare at him for a couple of seconds. "I'm not saying that I do want to be your girl, and I'm not saying that I don't want to be your girl, but you can't even ask me that if you haven't taken me on a date yet."

"Fair enough," he says. "I did invite you to dinner though."

"Uh-huh. Come on, let's go." We walk to the door and then head downstairs. He touches the side of my back and grabs my hand for a second.

"Hey, Ella," he says before we walk into the street.

I look up at him curiously. "Yeah?"

"I do like you, you know. You get that, right? It's not just about the sex or anything." He sounds slightly disjointed and I'm surprised because he's normally so confident.

"Hey, are you being serious right now?" I say, glancing at him.

"Yeah. Why?"

"I don't know. It's just weird. You're always joking around all the time."

"I just want you to know that this is special and we will have to tell your parents at some point, and Sam. If I survive past us telling them, then I want to take you on some real dates, you know?" He shrugs.

"No, I don't know. What does that mean?"

"We'll talk about it later," he says. I stare at him for a couple of seconds and my heart feels like it's soaring. Does he *like me*, like me? Is this about more than sex? Do I *like him*, like him? I already know the answer to that, but I'm not going to say anything. We get into the back of the car and the driver takes us over to Danny's. I can see Danny standing outside, and I frown. Why is he outside and not in the apartment?

"Stay here," I say to Colton. "Do not get out of the car. I won't be a minute."

Colton lets out a deep sigh. "This is not a good idea, Ella, but I'm going to listen to you."

"Thank you," I say as I slide out of the car. I head over to Danny. He walks over to me and gives me a big hug. He holds me a little too tightly for a little too long, but I just stand there. He must really be in need of someone.

He steps back. "Hey, thank you so much for coming over."

"It's okay. Is everything okay? How's Frannie?"

"Huh?" he says, blinking, staring at me.

"Is she okay? Was she crying about her mom or something?"

"No." He shakes his head. "Why would she be crying about her mom?"

"I mean, because I figured that's why you would really want to talk to me." I'm confused now. "What's going on, Danny? I don't understand why you called me."

"I was hoping that we could go somewhere," his voice deeper than I've ever heard before and a trickle of something ominous is creeping up my spine.

"What?" I know I sound like a bit of an idiot, just standing there, hoping beyond hope that this isn't going where I think it's going.

"I was hoping we could go somewhere."

"But what about Frannie?" I say, looking at him hard, desperately hoping Frannie will pop out and say, "Boo." And then we will all laugh like this is some big bad joke. It's not a particularly funny one, but then Danny's not exactly Adam Sandler.

"She's upstairs with a babysitter."

"A babysitter? Wait, what? I didn't realize you had several." I blink in confusion. Hadn't he once told me that I was the only person he trusted to look after Frannie?

"Of course," he says. "I had to find someone else if I also wanted this to be professional."

"What do you mean?" What on earth was he talking about? A dull ache pounded in my head and I had a feeling that something bad was about to happen.

"I mean, if we're going to start dating and fucking, then I don't want to complicate things by you also being her babysitter."

"What?" My jaw drops. Danny had just made a comment about us being together.

Sexually.

I'm in shock.

How could he have even thought such a thing?

Am I really that clueless? How could I not have seen this coming?

"I mean, you left your panties for me, Ella." He says the words as if they are turning him on and I realize that I'm an even bigger fool than I thought I was. How could one person be that slow?

"I didn't leave my panties for you. I—" I bite down on my lower lip. How can I tell him what really happened? "Look, it's just... I don't know how to explain this, but..."

"I know you want me. It's okay," he says as he grabs my hands and pulls me into him. "I want you too. You know how many months it's been since I fucked?" he says and my stomach curls.

I glance at him for a couple of seconds, trying to think of how I can respond without being extremely rude. I can't quite believe that this is actually happening. Danny is actually coming on to me. I can't believe I've been so blind. I soon realize that he is mistaking my silence for me being into it and I know I have to say something quickly.

"Now I'm going to give you the kiss," he says, but before he can say anything else, he's yanked away from me and I see Colton standing there. I've never been happier to see him in my life.

"Back the fuck off of my girl, Danny." I stare at Colton and he's glaring at me and Danny. I shudder at the look on his face. He's pissed as hell. "I told you this was a mistake, Ella, but would you listen to me?"

"Who the fuck are you?" Danny says, looking like he wants to take a shot at Colton. "What's going on here, Ella?"

"He gave me a ride over," I say as if that is explanation enough. "It's late." I shrug as I mumble. "I didn't want to take public transport."

"And you want to know why I gave her a ride over, Danny? Because I knew you were scum, and you want to know why I was able to get her over here so quickly? Because I was in her bed when you called. And you wanna know why I was in her bed? Because I just fucked her." Colton says the words slowly as if he's savoring them. "We're fucking. She's mine." He puts his arm around my waist. "So back the fuck off. You will never see her again, and unfortunately for your daughter, Frannie, she's never going to see her again either."

"No," I say, glaring at Colton and how he's talking like I'm his possession and he can dictate my life. "I am going to see her again. I love her. She deserves better than this." I stare at Danny. "I can't believe you. Your wife has already left you. Frannie has no one. I'm one of the closest people in her life and you're going to do this? You're going to jeopardize our relationship?"

"I thought you wanted me," he says, shaking his head. "You left your wet panties for me to find and—"

"She didn't leave her panties for you," Colton says grumpily. I don't know why he's acting so pissed off. He's the reason why my panties were off in the first place. "She took off her panties because she was playing with herself while I was on the phone with her and you came home, okay?"

"Actually, that's not exactly what—" I start, but Danny cuts me off.

"You were having phone sex at my house while you were babysitting?" Danny says, his jaw dropped and eyes wide. He's looking at me like I'm some deviant. "While I was paying you to look after my daughter, you were—"

"Oh, shut up," Colton says in a hard tone. I see Danny flinch and I can tell that he's worried that Colton is going to beat him up or something. I stare at Colton and his bulging muscles and I can't believe just how turned on I am in that moment. "Come on, Ella."

"I don't know what to say," I say, trying to find a way to make this situation better. "Look, Danny, I'm sorry. I know that was unprofessional, but..."

"You can see Frannie one last time," Danny says, looking at me with hurt and disgust on his face. "But as far as I'm concerned, this is over. You weren't even that great a babysitter in the first place."

"What?" I say, staring at him, hurt flooding through me at his words.

"You didn't even cook her any meals. All you ever did was get her pizza." He shakes his head. "You want her to turn into the pizza dough girl or something?" He scoffs. "It's just lazy."

I stare at him for a couple of seconds, not believing how he's speaking to me. "You never said it was a problem before."

"Maybe because I didn't care about your cooking." He looks me up and down. "But your pussy isn't worth all this drama."

"I should have known you were too good to be true." I press my lips together. "I thought you were a caring father and a good boss."

"I got a good cock." He chuckles. "If you ever get fed up with steroid boy there, feel free to take a ride on my baloney pony."

"I think I know we both know why his wife left him now," Colton says, his eyes searching mine. I can see that he's trying to figure out if I'm okay or if I'm going to start crying. I shake my head to let him know that I'm not going to break down. Now that I've seen this side of Danny, I will never be able to think about or look at him in the same way again.

"Good night, Danny," I say as Colton escorts me back to the vehicle. We get into the back of the car in silence and I stare out of the window. Shock has set in and I don't know what to say. The driver takes off and we go in a different direction from my apartment. "Where are we going?" I say.

"We're going back to my place," Colton says as if I've asked a stupid question.

"But..."

"But nothing," he says. "We're going back to my place and we're spending the night there." He turns to look at me. I know for sure he's going to say that he told me not to go over there, but he doesn't. He grabs my hand and holds it. We sit there in companionable silence for a couple of minutes and he looks over at me. "I'm sorry, you know."

"What are you sorry about?" I ask him, surprised by how kind he is being.

"I'm sorry that Danny turned out to be a jerk. I'm sorry that your relationship with Frannie has most probably ended now. I know how much that little girl meant to you. You're a good, kind person. I know that you wanted to be in her life. I know you wanted to be a mother figure to her, but you can't be the mother figure to her when you don't have that role with her father."

I nod slowly. I understand what he's saying, though I feel bad. "I just didn't expect any of this to go down like this," I say, shaking my head. "Though I guess I should have realized that something was wrong. There were many instances where it felt slightly off, but I just told myself I was imagining it."

"Like us?" He says softly and my eyes snap to his.

"What do you mean?"

"Do you think you're imagining the chemistry between us?"

I stare at him for a couple of seconds, my heart racing. "So you think there's chemistry between us?"

"I know there's chemistry between us. I've liked you for years. I know that we've had a combustious relationship, I know that you've disliked me ever since I fired you, but you know why I did it. Sam is my best friend and I would never want to jeopardize that relationship. I knew that all he wanted in his life was to protect you, and I knew that he might not approve, but now I don't care. You're old enough, and I think you like me."

"I mean, I maybe like you."

"I knew it was you at the party, Ella," he says. "I knew it was you the first moment I saw you. In fact, I only went to the party because Sam told me that you were going to be there."

"What?" I stare at him. My jaw drops. "You only went because I was going to be there?"

"I wanted to talk to you. It's been years and you've been avoiding me and I needed to see you."

"But I didn't even realize."

"I know," he says. "I've always been in love with you, Ella. It sounds weird to say that, but it's true. It's always been you."

"I had no clue." I stare at him in shock. I know that's not what he wants to hear, but I don't know what to say. Am I in love with him? What am I feeling for him? For so many years, I've been so annoyed and frustrated with him over what had happened in the past. Sure, the last couple of weeks have been amazing. The sex has been great, but I don't know if I love him. I don't know what this is.

"You don't have to say anything. I'm not asking you to declare your love to me. I'm just telling you, Ella, that it's always been you for me, you know."

"Is that why you said you were giving yourself to me as a present?" I roll my eyes.

"Hey, I was hoping that you'd say something like I was the best present you ever had in your life, but you didn't."

"You knew I wasn't going to say that."

"True," he says. "But I'm hoping one day all you'll want for Christmas is me."

24

One week later.

"I can't believe that he went on a work trip the very next day after he declared his love to me," I say to Isabel and Sarah as we sit at the steak restaurant eating dinner. I've spent every single night with the girls since my disastrous night with Zevo and Danny. Colton went out of town and I haven't seen him since that night and it is killing me.

"He's been texting you though, right?" Isabel asks as she sips on her wine.

"I mean, he texts me in the morning saying, 'Good morning. I hope you have a great day.' And then he texts me in the evening saying, 'Sweet dreams.' But that's it," I say, sitting back on the soft cushion. "I wish that he would call me or something."

"He's most probably feeling upset that you didn't tell him that you loved him back," Sarah says, shaking her head as if she can't believe I didn't confess my undying love to him then and there. "I mean, he confessed his feelings for you and you kind of just dissed him."

"I didn't diss him," I say, trying to defend myself. I've

spent the last couple of days questioning myself as to why I didn't tell him how I felt about him. I knew it was because I was nervous that everything wasn't real, but I hadn't been able to express that to anyone. "I was just overwhelmed. I didn't know what to think or feel."

"But you love him," Isabel says simply. "It's obvious."

"What do you mean it's obvious?" I say, blushing slightly.

"Girl, the fact that you went back to his place that first night even though you supposedly couldn't stand him."

I stare at her for a couple of seconds. "What are you saying?"

"I'm saying you've always had a thing for Colton Hart. Don't think I don't remember the night before the first time you were going to work for him."

"What are you talking about?" I say.

"You were going on and on about how hot he was. Remember?" I blush slightly. I do remember. Of course I remember. I've always had a thing for Colton. I've always thought of him as my brother's hot, hot friend, and I've been having fantasies about him for years. But after he fired me, I've tried to dismiss it because it is just so embarrassing.

"You love him," Isabel says. "And I know that you're slightly taken aback by how quickly everything has gone, but it's okay. He loves you too."

"I mean, how do I know it's real?" I ask. "He doesn't know me that well, and he hasn't even taken me on a date yet."

"I know. That is kind of weird," Sarah says. "I mean, not to be rude or anything, but you guys have fucked so much and you haven't even been on one date. It's like you guys are just friends with benefits but not even really friends."

"Thanks, Sarah. That makes me feel great."

"I'm just saying. It's not like I would turn it down. It is just a little bit weird."

"I mean, he did ask me to dinner that one time, but..." I sigh. My phone starts ringing and I see that Sam is calling. "Hey, hold on. It's Sam. Hey, what's going on?" I ask him.

"Hey, I just wanted to let you know that I know about you and Colton."

"What?" I ask, freezing.

"I know." Sam chuckles on the phone.

"What do you mean you know?"

"I know that you guys are dating," he says.

"Wait, how do you know?"

"Because Colton told me." He sighs. "I don't know why you didn't tell me in the first place."

"I mean, I just don't..." I don't know what to say. I can hear my words floundering.

"Colton helped Mom and Dad," he says, "and I feel slightly guilty about that because I didn't even know there was an issue."

"What are you talking about? What do you mean he helped Mom and Dad?"

"He's in Florida right now."

"He is?" I say. "I didn't know he was in Florida. I thought he was somewhere else."

"Dad lost money." Sam sounds annoyed. "He didn't want to tell us because he felt guilty, but he was investing his retirement money in some company that's gone bankrupt, and they're in a really bad way."

"Oh my gosh. I didn't know that."

"Colton has been helping them."

"He has? What?"

"I guess he has been putting money into a brokerage for them, and he's been managing it and adding money and"—he sounds frustrated—"I feel a little bit annoyed that Mom and Dad didn't tell me this. And I'm kind of annoyed at Colton because this isn't his responsibility, but I'm thankful that Mom and Dad trusted him enough to go to him."

"But why would he do that? Why would he help them?"

"Well, that's what I was wondering myself," Sam says. "I went off on him when I found out."

"Oh?" I say. "You didn't know?"

"Of course I didn't know." He's angry now. "So I asked him why, and he told me it was because he was in love with you. And because he's in love with you, he wants to take care of Mom and Dad as well."

"Oh," I say, shocked that Colton had told Sam that he was in love with me. "I didn't know he was doing this, Sam. Really, I didn't even know Mom and Dad were in trouble."

"I know," he says. "They didn't tell anyone aside from him." He sighs. "Anyway, I just want you to know that you have my blessing."

"I do?"

"I know Colton. He's like a brother to me. He's one of the best guys I know."

"But you always said that he was a player and that..."

"Doesn't mean a player can't settle down," Sam says, laughing. "Anyway, just wanted you to know that I know, so you don't have to hide things from me. Okay, sis?"

"I know."

"I'm here for you."

"I know."

"I just want to make sure you know because Mom and Dad obviously didn't think I was going to be there for them, so I want you to know you can come to me at any time."

"Thank you," I say and hang up. I look over at Isabel and Sarah, who are staring at me with wide eyes. "Guys, you are not going to believe what's going on. But one second." I text Colton.

Me: Thank you. I miss you.

He texts me back immediately.

Colton: Finally. I've been waiting for you to say that you miss me.

I just smile at the text.

Isabel glances at me. "What is going on?"

"Colton is the perfect guy," I say. "He really is. He's been..." I pause as I notice a guy heading toward us with a guitar. I blink and sit back. Sarah and Isabel look around and their jaws drop. The guy starts singing an Ed Sheeran song, one of my favorite songs, and then he hands me a dozen red roses. "Are you sure these are for me?" I blink.

"You're Ella, right?" he says.

"Yeah."

"They're for you." He continues playing the song, and I can feel my heart racing. Then I see someone coming up behind him. My heart freezes when I see it's Colton. He's wearing a black suit with a red tie, and there's a goofy grin on his face. He has a bow on his head and we start laughing.

"Hey," he says.

"Hey," I say back. "What is going on?"

"Well, I thought that I would surprise you."

"But how did you know I was here? Wait, I'm confused." I look at him, and then I hear Isabel giggling nervously. I glance over at her and she shrugs.

"I'm sorry," she says, "I told him you were going to be here."

"But wait, what?"

"I got her number from Sam," Colton says, grinning. "I texted her because I wanted to surprise you and I wanted to know where you were."

"You told him we were going to be at this diner?" I asked her.

"Yeah. I don't stand in the way of true love," she says. She grabs Sarah. "Come on, let's go."

"But I wanted to witness this. This might be the most romantic thing I've ever seen in my life," Sarah says, and Isabel starts laughing.

"Don't worry. You and I will have our moments one day

too." Isabel gives me a big smile and then turns to Colton. "I'll see you both later."

"Thanks, Isabel," he says, squeezing her hand, and I can tell that he will always have a soft spot for her in his heart. He takes her seat, gives the guy who was serenading me some money, and then looks across at me. "Are you mad?" he asks, his eyes searching mine. As if I could ever be mad at him for more than a few seconds.

"No. I'm just really shocked."

"I'm sure you are. I've never seen you this speechless before."

"Very funny, Colton. I didn't even know you were back in town."

"I was just waiting for you to tell me that you missed me," he says.

"But what if I never told you that I missed you? Would you still have come tonight?"

"Maybe, maybe not." He laughs. "I just was hoping that perhaps you would miss me enough to text me and tell me that."

"You know what, Colton Hart?" I ask, taking a deep breath.

"No. What?"

"I used to think that all I wanted for Christmas was not you." I giggle. "But I was so wrong. I love you. You have my whole heart. You have my entire being, and I feel absolutely crazy for saying that because we've never been on an official date. But you're just kind of great. You know that?"

"I was hoping you'd say that." He leans forward and grabs my hands. "I was also hoping you'd say you'd be my girl."

"But..."

"But nothing," he says. "And I have a special present for you."

"What's the special present? Please don't tell me that it's your big cock in the bathroom."

"No, but that could be arranged." He chuckles, and I stare at the dimples in his cheeks. "No, I was thinking for our first official date, I take you to Paris."

"Paris, France?"

"Yeah," he says, his eyes light with mirth. "Does that sound good?"

"Yeah." Which is an understatement. My heart is jumping for joy. I want to throw my arms around him and kiss him and tell him that a trip to Paris was the most romantic first date a girl could ever ask for.

"Great. So how's about we go back to my place now, and then tomorrow we hop on a plane for France?"

"Tomorrow? But we have work and..."

"No, we don't," he says as he opens his briefcase and pulls out a stack of brochures. He hands them to me and I frown. Was this really the place for us to be discussing work?

I stare at the front and see one of my logos. "What is this?" I ask, my heart thudding in pride.

"This is the one we went for. It's official," he says, a confident grin on his handsome face. "All of our official documents will have this branding."

"But I didn't even get to do the other drafts. I..."

"It was perfect just as it was," he says, pressing a finger to my lips. "Just like you. This work comes naturally to you. Your designs were amazing."

"Are you being serious right now?" I'm shocked at how sweet he is being. "Are you pulling my leg?"

"Never." He grins. "I love you, Ella. I've always loved you. And while this is a very unconventional start to a dating relationship, that's okay because we're unconventional. All I know is that I want to be with you. All I know is that I want to spoil you and help you find your way, help you find the things that you love to do. I just want you to live the best life that you can. All I ask is that you let me go on that journey with you."

"You're amazing. You know that, right?" My voice is breathless and I'm trying to explain to him just how much he means to me. But sometimes, there just aren't words to express how full and happy your heart is. Sometimes, there aren't adequate words to explain to someone how much joy they fill you with. It's an amazing and scary feeling to feel that much love for someone.

"I mean, I like to think I'm okay," he says, laughing slightly. He shifts his chair over so he's next to me and gives me a kiss on the lips. "You are my absolute joy in life, Ella. Being with you, well, it will never be dull."

"You can say that again, especially when we have masks on." I think back to that night at Sam's work party. "That was one of the most exciting nights I've ever had."

"Then I guess we need to have masks on again, real quick." He grins. "I quite like the idea of being on another dance floor, having my wicked way with you."

"Oh my gosh, really?" I ask, giggling. "That night was crazy."

"Maybe because I'm crazy about you. You know what, Ella?"

"What, Colton?"

"All I want for Christmas is you, and it looks like I've been lucky enough to get the present I've waited my entire life for."

"I love you," I say as I pull him toward me and kiss him deeply. His fingers run through my hair and I can feel my heart aching to be closer to him. "Let's go back to your place," I whisper against his lips.

"Oh?" He asks as if he doesn't know what I want.

"I mean, unless you don't have any condoms," I say with a giggle. "Because this assistant is off for the night and not about to pick some up for you."

"Well, you don't have to worry about that." He growls and pulls me onto his lap so I can feel his hardness beneath me. "'Cause I have a feeling that we won't be needing any soon."

It's my turn to say, "Oh," and I tremble slightly as his fingers slip between my legs. He bites the side of my neck and grunts as I reach down and rub his cock.

"Keep that up and we'll be fucking right here at the table in front of everyone." He grunts as he turns me to the side and kisses me again. "Not that I mind, of course, but I have a feeling you might."

"How considerate you are," I say, giggling.

"It's because I love you so," he says as he grabs my hand and places it on his heart. "You own this now, Ella, my darling. Please be gentle with it."

"I will, my love," I say softly. "I promise that I will never let it go."

And for a few moments we stare at each other, our eyes screaming our love for each other. I am not sure I have ever been happier than I am in this moment.

"I guess we both got what we wanted this Christmas." He taps the tip of my nose and then kisses me. "True love and happiness, I don't think I could have wished for anything more."

Thank you for reading All I Want For Christmas is Not You! If you would like to enjoy a free bonus chapter from Colton's POV, please click here!

The next book following these friends is Mid Thirties Slightly Hot Mess Female Seeking Billionaire, starring Sarah!

mid-thirties slightly hot mess female seeking billionaire

New York Times Bestselling Author
J. S. COOPER

To Whom it May Concern,

This is a long shot.

I'm seeking a billionaire, I will also settle for a millionaire. Sorry, not interested in any salesmen looking to sell me a timeshare or a part of their animal balloon company (been there, done that).

I am not a golddigger, though you may not believe that. I have references. Ask all of my broke exes and my best friend.

To be fair, I am not a glamorous model, actress, or professional dancer. I do, however, take pole dancing lessons (for fun, of course, not dollar bills).

I am an educated (still have the student loans to prove it), open-minded (toy stores are fun, and not for games), fairly cute (when I try), only a little curvy (those last 30 lbs don't want to leave) single female. I want to be swept off of my feet, wined, dined, and bedded in ways that make me forget my own name.

I have a job (that I hate), with a boss that makes me want to jump off of a cliff. However, my friends make up for the day job. I'm ready for an adventure. And possibly a penthouse with a maid and a design budget.

If interested, please respond before Monday morning, so I don't have to go into work.

Love,
Sultry Sassy Sarah
***

Note to self: Don't write stupid ads while half drunk and hanging out with immature obnoxious friends. Certainly do not post them on the internal company message thread by mistake. Do not freak out when your boss says he wants to see you in the office first thing Monday morning. And please never make a joke asking how many dollar bills he has to make it rain ever again.

I'm dead meat.

Preorder here!

ACKNOWLEDGMENTS

Thank you to my beta readers Andrea Robinson, Meagen Campbell, Ashley Grindstaff, Sharon Boldt, Bobbie, Pamela Nunn, Heather Menna, Randi Goff, Donna Veilleux, Michelle Norberg, Vickie Komarek, Trina, and Meagan Montgomery. I appreciate all your help and feedback on this book.

To all the readers, thank you for taking time out to read my Christmas book. I really hope you enjoyed it and had a couple of laughs!

I had a really fun time writing this book. I look forward to writing more steamy romcoms in 2024!

Lots of love,

Jaimie AKA J. S. AKA Natalia! :)

J. S. stands for Jaimie Suzi and Natalia is the penname I created for my mafia romance books!

XOXO

If you want to stay connected with me, you can find me here:

Facebook

Instagram

Tiktok

Or you can email me at jscooperauthor@gmail.com.